"I've got you."

Jamie reached down and hauled Shaylee up to safety.

The loud pounding of her heart nearly blocked the unrelenting gunfire. Shaylee and Jamie crouched, flattening themselves against the rock.

Jamie reined in Bugsy, holding her by the handle on her vest. She continued barking wildly. "Shh," he admonished, pulling the dog closer. She quieted with a throaty growl.

The shooting ceased as quickly as it had begun.

"Is he gone?" Jamie whispered.

"Just wait." Shaylee stared toward the trees, searching for the mysterious shooter.

Impatience and curiosity won out, and Shaylee started to rise.

A bullet pelted the stone, and she ducked again.

Jamie cast a look at her. "Where is he?"

"I don't know, but he's got us trapped."

Sharee Stover is a Colorado native transplanted to Nebraska, where she lives with her husband, three children and two dogs. Her mother instilled in her a love of books before Sharee could read, along with the promise "if you can read, you can do anything." When she's not writing, she enjoys time with her family, long walks with her obnoxiously lovable German shepherd and crocheting. Find her at shareestover.com or on Twitter, @shareestover.

Books by Sharee Stover

Love Inspired Suspense

Secret Past
Silent Night Suspect
Untraceable Evidence
Grave Christmas Secrets
Cold Case Trail
Tracking Concealed Evidence

Visit the Author Profile page at LoveInspired.com.

TRACKING
CONCEALED
EVIDENCE

SHAREE STOVER

LOVE INSPIRED SUSPENSE
INSPIRATIONAL ROMANCE

LOVE INSPIRED SUSPENSE
INSPIRATIONAL ROMANCE

ISBN-13: 978-1-335-55490-1

Recycling programs
for this product may
not exist in your area.

Tracking Concealed Evidence

This edition published by arrangement with Harlequin Books S.A.

For questions and comments about the quality of this book, please contact us
at CustomerService@Harlequin.com.

Love Inspired
22 Adelaide St. West, 41st Floor
Toronto, Ontario M5H 4E3, Canada
www.LoveInspired.com

Printed in U.S.A.

For the invisible things of him from the creation of the world are clearly seen, being understood by the things that are made, even his eternal power and Godhead; so that they are without excuse.
—*Romans* 1:20

Father God, thank you for the beauty of creation
to illustrate Your life-changing Word.
All glory and honor belong to You alone.

ONE

An eerie howl clawed at the edges of Shaylee Adler's consciousness, dragging her from the depths of darkness. She struggled to open her eyes, uncertain why they felt so heavy. She reached to touch her face, the effort straining as though quicksand held her submerged in its grasp.

At last, lifting her hand, she slapped the back of her knuckles against a hard surface overhead. With determination, she forced her eyelids open.

Quick scratching echoed, beckoning her to wake.

She groaned.

The floor seemed to spin beneath her.

Arms tight against her sides, Shaylee willed herself to sit up, but her body refused to cooperate. She blinked, fighting the comfortable lure of sleep. The scratching continued, sending an involuntary shudder through her.

Movement above caught her attention, and the object shifted with a thud, shaking her. Another series of quick, raking grates, followed by high-pitched howls, spurred her fully conscious.

Daggered claws attached to enormous paws hovered over her face.

Shaylee's arms flew up in protection and she attempted to scramble away, unable to move in the confining space. She screamed, bolting—unsuccessfully—upright and smacked her forehead on the strange low ceiling, startling the animal. He disappeared from the invisible barrier mercifully separating them. Shaylee flattened her palm against the plastic.

An ear-piercing howl in the distance sent shivers radiating through her body.

With her fingers, Shaylee roamed the space, tracing mere inches between her and the straight-edged walls surrounding her on every side. She couldn't roll over or sit up. Instead, she lay on her back, the hard, unforgiving floor beneath her.

The atmosphere was warm and thick. Her mind raced with possibilities, continually returning to the most terrifying scenario.

She dared not linger or entertain the thought.

A tiny red light near her feet blinked.

Panic tightened her chest.

Shaylee squeezed her eyes closed, inhaling slowly to calm herself against the terror of being trapped, which consumed her senses.

She reached for her phone, then remembered she'd left it on the kitchen counter while making her nightly chamomile tea. Then what had happened? She couldn't remember anything after that. Mentally reversing images, she recalled going to Baxter's house and interrupting his dinner party with the ripped portion of the accounting journal she'd found in Zia's Bible. She hadn't gotten far before his bodyguard threw her out. She'd driven around for a couple of hours before going home, making her tea and then pacing her kitchen to calm herself after the encounter with Baxter. Had she settled onto the sofa? Everything after arriving home was a complete blank.

Her head ached, and fear loomed stronger than ever. Why was her brain so foggy?

Once more she traced the confined space, her hands moving faster now, frantically searching for an escape.

She pressed her palms against the smooth wall overhead, but it didn't budge.

"No. No." The words slipped from her lips. Tiny protests unheard by anyone but her.

A tickle on her ear had Shaylee instinctively swiping and smacking her hand on the ceiling. An insect skittered across her forehead.

She refused to release the scream threatening to erupt and drag her into hysteria. Instead, Shaylee stretched to her full length, pressing her feet against the unmoving wall. Something poked her thigh. Her keys. She had a flashlight on her keyring!

Recalling she hadn't taken off her boots or cleaned out her pockets when she'd gotten home, Shaylee was almost grateful for the agitation of dealing with Baxter that had kept her from getting too comfortable for the night. Shaylee slid her arm down, focused on the activity and not her terrifying circumstances. Reaching into the side pocket of her cargo pants, she grazed the familiar object. She looped the ring around her forefinger and tugged it free. Dragging it onto her stomach, she used her other hand to activate the light and then brought it upward.

At last, a small beam illuminated the space. Thick plexiglass walls encased her, and dark brown earth pressed against the sides. Above her, slivers of moonlight were visible through the sporadically swiped dirt. The realization slammed into her with the impact of a semitruck.

She was buried alive!

Desperate, she pounded on the ceiling with all her strength. "Help! Somebody, help me!"

Movement above her.

Someone was out there. Hope and boldness fueled Shaylee's cries. With fury, she added kicks to her attack on the ceiling. "Here! I'm down here!"

A strange scuffle and the enormous paws returned, bearing the weight of the equally gigantic creatures. Pausing, she shifted the light. Two sets of looming jaws gazed down at her.

Coyotes!

With a gasp, she lowered her arms, shrinking back, and held up the minuscule light. "Lord, make them go away!"

The animals seemed to study her, aware their prize lay just below the clear plastic barrier. Wild and skilled at extracting their prey, they wouldn't allow anything to interrupt their focused exercise.

Terror constricted Shaylee's chest, enveloping her in a stranglehold. Throat tight, she wheezed, forcing bursts of air in and out of her lungs. Instinct reminded her that she'd hyperventilate if she continued to panic.

Pray. The prodding thought came as natural as her next panting breath. Shaylee forced herself to inhale and exhale slowly, calming herself. Conserve the oxygen, or suffocation would kill her before help arrived.

And help would arrive. -

It had to.

"Thank You, Lord, for the plastic separating me from the coyotes. You see me, even now. I trust You," she whispered the prayer through parched lips.

Doubt, like a hissing whisper, mocked, *Does God see you?* Would rescue come? After all no one, including Shaylee, had protected and rescued her sister, Zia, from her conniving husband, Baxter Heathcote.

Tears welled and burned.

If she died, would they find her buried here? Where was she?

Would her life be erased, just like Zia's?

Who would investigate her death the way Shaylee obsessively worked to prove Baxter was her sister's murderer?

Nobody.

More howling.

Closer this time.

The hairs on Shaylee's arms rose in terror.

"Help, someone, please!"

Undeterred by her desperate cries, the animals worked together, furiously scratching at the surface. They growled, snarling warnings until the coyote directly above Shaylee gripped something red and tugged it free. Enticed, his friends scurried off to join him in consuming the prize.

Several long silent seconds passed. Unable to move, Shaylee blinked and flexed her hands, confirming she was still alive.

"Thank You, Lord." She sucked in a breath, focused again on her imprisonment, and surveyed her boundaries.

But no help had arrived.

No rescue workers.

Only darkness encroached on her from every angle.

Resignation smothered her as a bug wriggled near her eye. She would die tonight.

Shaylee tried to swallow against her barren throat, now sore from her pleas. Her body shook with adrenaline convulsions.

Before she could restrain it, a primal scream erupted from deep within her, shattering the silence.

Dear God, save me! I'm buried alive.

Jamey Dyer and his cadaver dog, Bugsy, fully intended to defy the guards who had prohibited his entrance into the Black Hills National Forest. Jamey wasn't a rule breaker. Quite the opposite. However, his justification for trespassing was the same reason the state had cordoned off the area as a danger zone. Namely, the gaping and unpredictable sinkhole that had recently exposed an old gypsum mine underground, which proved Jamey's initial theory about the murder of Zia Heathcote. And this time, he and Bugsy would find the woman, who he suspected was buried nearby.

He didn't allow himself a moment to debate whether this was the right decision. The beginning rays of sunrise peeked over the horizon, urging him on. Not a moment to waste.

Jamey focused on keeping out of sight and moving as quickly as possible to reach the backside of the massive rock formations that would hide him and Bugsy from the main road. They had to get to higher ground to evaluate the topography of the sinkhole. Once he got a bird's-eye view, he'd know where to start the search. The need to remain concealed meant staying off the hiking path.

Jamey kept Bugsy beside him, not yet allowing her to work the full length of her leash. As if she understood the importance of speed and discretion, she remained close.

They moved together in sync, climbing and weaving through the terrain, and crested the mountain. He paused at the edge of the cliff with nothing between himself and the treacherous drop to the floor of the rocky valley below. Infusing his lungs with the crisp morning air, Jamey allowed his gaze to travel the beauty of South Dakota's Black Hills, marveling at the gorgeous display before him. "Lord, You do amazing work."

Craggy cliffs stretched toward the boundless sky, painted in brilliant shades of cerulean, rose and lavender. They transitioned into the warm citrus orange and welcoming yellow of the rising sun. The mountainous land expanded in a sporadic line of varying heights, like notes on a page of music. Green bushes dotted the white rocky ground and granite spires reached high from where their bedding planes marked time with definitive lines.

Always in tune with her handler, Bugsy sat beside him, reporting for duty. He knelt and stroked the bluetick coonhound's velvet floppy ears. "Are you ready to work today?"

She gazed up at him with soulful brown eyes, tail wagging.

"Glad to hear it," Jamey joked in the one-sided conversation.

Bugsy had proven herself a trustworthy companion, always maintaining his confidence and holding his secrets. In return, he allowed her to take the spotlight whenever they worked recovery missions. Truthfully, Jamey preferred staying behind the scenes. He'd had enough unwanted attention and the painful consequences that came with notoriety to last him a lifetime.

Jamey slid his backpack off his shoulders and double-checked his cell phone—void of service in the remote location, as expected. He withdrew the binoculars and surveyed the landscape, spotting the sinkhole. It was much larger than he'd anticipated, and they'd have to approach from the farthest side opposite the road. He visually roved to where the old suspension bridge hung. Perfect, not visible from where the guards stood, and the passage provided the quickest way across.

Bugsy waited patiently, scratching her ear with her hind leg. Jamey dropped the binoculars into the bag and grasped her cadaver gear, then reconsidered. The bright orange vest might draw unwanted attention from the guards. Instead, he selected her black vested harness. As soon as she spotted the accessory, she sat upright, ears perked.

Time to work.

Jamey chuckled as he slid the material over her, securing the clasps, then snapped the twenty-foot hands-free leash. He secured one end to her collar and the other to his belt. Then, gripping the length of the tether, he reined

Bugsy close to his side until he released her to search. "All right, Bugs, let's do this."

Sporadic sprouts of wildflowers, scraggly bushes and hardy grass tufts littered the uneven ground. They traversed the rocky terrain to the old suspension bridge. Jamey paused briefly, glancing at the Bridge Closed warning sign. He assessed the structure, aware it was in decent shape since he and Bugsy had worked the mountain many times. The park regularly closed the bridge for required maintenance, not because it posed a danger.

Jamey and Bugsy approached. The planks and ropes were strong, so he didn't fear falling through. Bugsy's wary expression proved how necessary daily training was for her. A cadaver dog needed to brave the environment and landscape whatever the condition.

"Come on, girl. You've done this before," Jamey gently encouraged, tugging on her leash and forcing Bugsy to keep up with him as they made their way to the other side.

Once they'd stepped off the bridge and onto solid ground, he loosened the leash, giving her the full twenty feet to work. "Bugsy."

She halted, faced him and waited, floppy ears at attention.

"Seek Adam." He used the command *Adam* to reinforce what her training vest indicated, search for human remains.

Whiskers twitching, she turned and headed east with a steady gait. Within moments, Bugsy was off, nose to the path, scurrying almost faster than Jamey could keep up. She'd slow, repeat the action, then continue.

They traveled farther than he'd planned, but he enjoyed the outdoors and didn't mind the lengthy hike.

Rough terrain and cracked earth split the ground in places. His shoes crunched the gravel and pine needles as they traversed higher up the mountain. Jamey and Bugsy had worked several cases in Nebraska and South Dakota, making them an experienced team.

Bugsy headed into a patch of thick foliage and dense bushes, advancing without hesitation, and edged her way into the thicket. Jamey hurried behind, ducking low-hanging branches and stepping over shrubs in a strange, bobbing dance. Finally, Bugsy aimed for disturbed ground.

She dropped to a sit, alerting. Had she found Zia?

Excited, but unwilling to reward her until he'd confirmed, he said, "Bugsy, find Adam."

She rose and clawed at the dirt, scratching her nails on something hard. Strips of red cloth lay scattered, and large paw prints encircled the freshly disturbed land.

Jamey inched closer, disbelieving. A partially exposed acrylic box—a coffin of sorts. Fog inside concealed many of the details of the encased body.

He dropped beside Bugsy and frantically brushed away the earth with his hands. Was it Zia?

Long scratches on the top indicated animal activity. Something had tried hard to get to whoever was inside. Thankfully, without success.

Jamey dug around the softened dirt until he found the latch and released it, then pulled open the lid. He fell back onto his behind, stunned. The woman inside had rosy cheeks and sweat beaded along her forehead. Perspiration matted her dark hair, splayed and concealing her face. Placing his fingers against her still warm neck, he sighed with relief and confusion, detecting a faint pulse.

"Please be okay." Jamey lifted her out of the coffin and set her down gently. He leaned close and listened for breaths. A soft flutter against his ear confirmed shallow breathing.

He turned the woman to her side, extending one arm above her head, the other tucked beneath her, then stretched one leg straight, keeping the other slightly bent to bear her weight in the recovery position.

"Lord, please help her wake up," he prayed, reaching for his phone, though he already knew he'd have no coverage. He rubbed her back in a firm, circular motion. "Come on, come on."

In a gasp, she jerked and launched into a coughing fit. She shifted into a crawl, then sat with her knees up.

"You're okay. You're safe." He watched intently for any signs of distress.

At last, the spasm passed, and she inhaled deeply.

"Good. Keep taking deep breaths."

She did as he suggested. Jamey reached into his backpack and removed a bottle of water. Twisting off the cap, he extended the offering.

Her wary expression and hesitation faded as she took the bottle.

"Drink slowly—" His words went unheeded as she guzzled, sending her into another fit of coughing.

She shoved the water at him and regained her composure. "Thank you."

"Sorry, I should've warned you before you drank."

"I'm so thirsty I wasn't thinking." Long hair hung in wild wisps around her face. She swept away the raven strands, revealing wide hazel eyes.

Recognition sucked the air from his lungs. No. It couldn't be her. Anybody but her. Detective Shaylee Adler, Zia Heathcote's sister.

"I know you... You're... Bug Dude." Shaylee's tone hinted a notch above condescending, and something flashed in her eyes.

He cringed at the unwanted nickname law enforcement had tagged him with after the trial. "Jamey Dyer, and this is my partner, Bugsy."

"Detective Shaylee Adler," she said, introducing herself as though that was news to him.

"Yes, I know." He spat the words with the bitterness of melted aspirin.

She appeared unfazed by his disdainful reply.

"Where am I?" Her gaze moved past him to the hole. Jumping to her feet, she backed against the closest tree, her hand slapping her hip. Searching for her gun? "Don't hurt me. I won't tell anyone. Just let me go."

Jamey blinked, processing the bizarre accusation. He scurried to stand and gestured at Bugsy, calmly waiting beside him. "You think I buried you? No. What? No. My dog, Bugsy, she found you. I tried to call the police, but I don't have cell reception." He held up his phone to emphasize his tumbled mess of confused, staccato explanation.

Shaylee jerked to focus on Bugsy, as though seeing her for the first time. "You're a search and rescue team, too?"

Jamey winced. "Um, sort of. We're more on the recovery side of things. Bugsy is a forensic detection dog."

"A cadaver dog? As in dead people?" Her mouth gaped in disbelief.

"Yeah, that's the strange thing. She's not trained for live people. And you're alive." Well, that just sounded dumb all the way around. "I mean, I'm not sure what drew her here."

Shaylee wrapped herself in a hug, and a glimmer of sunlight bounced from the badge attached to her belt.

Jamey stiffened at the reminder of her credentials. Of all the days to find a woman buried in a coffin. His rotten track record in working with law enforcement meant she'd probably arrest him for saving her life. He blinked. And for trespassing. Ugh. "Did you see your attacker? Why would someone bury you?"

Shaylee stared at him. "I don't remember much of anything prior to waking up in that—" She gestured at the coffin.

Despite the trauma, she looked pretty good. Jamey shook off the thought. Neither the hour nor the place. He awkwardly held out the bottle of water again, keeping a distance. She took the offering with the cautiousness of handling a live snake.

He brushed the dirt off his jeans. Now what?

Tension hung between them.

A slight breeze fluttered the overhead leaves, and Jamey studied the moss growing on the trunk of a nearby ponderosa pine.

Shaylee seemed to survey the thick forest bountiful in trees, bushes and underbrush except for the small clearing where the grave had been dug. "Where are we?"

"Black Hills National Forest."

Another awkward pause.

"We'll have to hike to my truck. There's no cell reception out here." She lifted an eyebrow, and Jamey wondered if she'd take off running. He almost hoped she would, then glanced down, feeling a pang of guilt for his not very nice thoughts. "Or you can find your way out alone. However, it goes faster with her." He squatted to pet Bugsy.

"That makes sense."

Jamey turned, his gaze dropping to the coffin again. Who would do something so heinous? He stepped beside it and noticed the insect in the bottom corner of the box. Dead. "Now, what are you doing in there," he mumbled.

Shaylee's footsteps drew closer. "Don't touch anything!"

He jerked to look at her and rolled his eyes. "Yes, I know."

"Sorry." She frowned. "What are you doing?"

Jamey knelt and sat back on his heels. *"Blattella germanica."*

"I beg your pardon?" Shaylee peered past him to the coffin.

"German cockroach."

"What?" She moved around him, glancing down. "Ew. That must've been what skittered over my face last night." She shivered. "So gross."

"And uncommon to be traveling alone." Jamey glanced away. *Good going, big mouth.* Law enforcement circles were small. After Heathcote's acquittal, Jamey had become a joke in every agency.

"You're Bug Dude, and you're a cadaver dog handler now?"

"Forensic entomologist," Jamey deliberately clarified the title in the hope she'd stop using the dreaded nickname. Focused on the insect, he continued, "Bugsy and I have worked as a forensic detection team for a long time."

A red light blinked at the foot of the coffin, and he visually traced a clear plastic wire to a small black box buried and disguised in the dirt. "What's this?" He snapped pictures with his cell phone, capturing as much of the scene as possible.

Shaylee coughed again, pressing her hand against her chest.

Jamey jumped to his feet. "We need to get you medical attention."

Bugsy gave a muffled *mrff,* then hurried to the edge of the clearing. Her hackles raised, she emitted a low growl.

"What's wrong?" The responding gunshot absorbed Jamey's question.

TWO

A whizzing sound past her ear sent Shaylee diving for cover and landing squarely on a prickly bush. Instinctively, she reached for her gun, then remembered she had no weapon.

The muffled gunfire had her rolling off the plant, arms sheltering her head in search of a place to hide. A boulder—at least five feet high and four feet wide, standing precariously close to the cliff's edge—provided the only viable option.

She made eye contact with Jamey and pointed to the rock. He gave a quick nod before another shot propelled them toward safety.

Shaylee reached the boulder first and rounded it, but not before skidding on the sandy ground.

Her right foot slid off the cliff.

Shaylee screamed and flung her arms out, grasping desperately for something to stop her fall.

As her fingers dug into the hard earth, her body slammed against the rocks. She clung for life, pressing the toe of her boot into a cleft.

Gravel cascaded around her. She turned and gasped at the cavernous drop to sharp rock formations beneath her.

Strong hands clamped her wrists. "I've got you." Jamey reached down and hauled her up to safety.

The loud pounding of her heart nearly blocked the unrelenting gunfire. With less than three feet of ledge between them and the precipice, Shaylee and Jamey crouched, flattening themselves against the rock.

Jamey reined in Bugsy, holding her by the handle on her vest. She continued barking wildly. "Shh," he admonished, pulling the dog closer. She quieted with a throaty growl.

The shooting ceased as quickly as it had begun.

"Is he gone?" Jamey whispered.

"Just wait." Shaylee stared toward the trees, searching for the mysterious shooter.

Seconds turned into minutes with no sign of the attacker. Impatience and curiosity won out, and Shaylee started to rise.

A bullet pelted the stone, flinging fragments, and she ducked again.

Jamey cast her a look that was somewhere between concern and agitation. "Where is he?"

"I don't know, but he's got us trapped."

He peered around the side of the boulder.

"Can you see anything?"

Another pop and he returned to crouching. "No."

A bullet hit the ground next to Shaylee. She tucked her feet in closer. "We can't sit here forever."

A rapid-fire series of shots consumed the air in response. Based on the succession of muffled sounds, Shaylee could tell the attacker was using a semiautomatic rifle with a silencer. But why bother in the mountains?

Bugsy barked and growled while Jamey kept her restrained beside him.

Shards of rock, stone and dirt rained on them. Fury and indignation overrode Shaylee's fear, but she prayed for wisdom since they had no weapons to retaliate with.

Finally, the shooting ceased.

Bugsy quieted.

Shaylee blinked and turned, startled to see Jamey staring at her. "Are we dead?"

She grinned despite the serious circumstances. "No. But don't move. Let him believe he succeeded." Shaylee's pulse drummed in her ears, and she struggled to listen for movement over the heavy bass beat consuming her senses. When no other shots pinged, she peered around the boulder.

"Is it safe?"

Shaylee pressed a finger to her lips.

Bugsy remained silent as if she understood.

Jamey started to move out from the cover. Shaylee gripped his forearm, the muscle surprisingly taut beneath her fingertips. "You can't rush out there. He might be waiting to finish the job."

"So we sit here and wait for him to pick us off like cans on a fence?"

"Great, hand me your gun and we'll shoot our way out of hiding."

"Point taken."

A rustle and Bugsy took off, barking.

"Bugsy!"

Shaylee jumped up as Jamey sprinted after the dog.

Both disappeared through the trees.

"Bugsy!" His frantic tone carried to her.

Had the shooter hurt the animal? Quickening her pace, Shaylee started after them, then spotted the dog bounding toward her. Exhaling relief, she knelt and petted Bugsy.

"She chased off whoever it was," Jamey huffed. His cheeks were flushed, and the leash dangled from his hand.

"What a brave girl," Shaylee praised.

"That's not like her. I'm just grateful he didn't turn and fire at her. How did the shooter know we were here? Did he return to finish you off?"

Her gaze roamed as she walked the perimeter of the

grave, intentionally keeping a distance. "Was he watching me?" A shiver ran through her.

Jamey spun to face Shaylee. "Yes! That's it!"

Before she responded, he rushed past her to the foot of the coffin and got down on his hands and knees. Shaylee joined him, intrigued by the small box he pointed out buried outside the coffin.

Jamey glanced up. Sunlight glimmered off his blue eyes. "This light is attached to the self-contained game camera."

Shaylee moved closer, above it and hopefully out of the line of the lens. She spotted the blinking red spot, then shifted to the side. "But it's not plugged into anything."

Jamey took off his backpack, pulled his hoodie off over his head and placed it at an angle over the camera, blocking the view. "It runs on a battery and SD card. I don't want to mess with the crime scene in case the investigators find something that'll help identify the criminal. We're not allowing him to watch any more, either."

"Does it have audio?" Shaylee whispered.

"Hmm, not sure." Jamey lowered his voice, then stood and ushered her away from the grave. "Do you have any idea who did this?"

Shaylee gritted her teeth. "Yeah, I do." Baxter Heathcote was behind this attack, but he'd never dirty his own hands to kill her. Jamey was a stranger and there was no need to drag him in any more than he'd already become involved in the matter.

"Why would someone want you dead?" Jamey considered her, his eyes unwavering.

"It's a long story."

She saw no judgment, only curiosity and concern. Interestingly, he didn't press for information. Instead, Jamey reached into his jeans pocket and removed his cell phone, then held it up, rotating the device to the right and left. He frowned, then walked to the edge of the cliff where the land sloped dangerously into the valley below. "Still no service. They invent machines to do everything known to man, but reception in the mountains remains unachievable."

He tucked the cell into his pocket. "We'll have to hike to my truck. I'm parked at least a mile away, and it's difficult terrain."

She had no reason to trust Jamey, except that he'd rescued her, and his dog was sweet. She also didn't relish the idea of traipsing unfamiliar territory alone while a faceless maniac tried to kill her. Besides, where would she go? Without a vehicle, her only option was hitchhiking once she reached the highway. Not smart. She groaned and swept her out-of-control, matted hair away from her face.

"Detective Adler?"

"Shaylee, please. And sorry, I was contemplating my lack of options." Unintended sarcasm laced her comment, and judging by Jamey's frown, she'd hurt his feelings. "Let's do this before the shooter returns."

He seemed to survey her. "Are you sure you're strong enough to make the hike? I could carry you." His tall, thin stature held a confidence, and the definition of his well-developed biceps and triceps—now visible through the athletic shirt he wore—testified to regular workouts. Glimpses of silver peppered his hair, and even his wire-framed glasses were classy, giving him an academic persona.

Shaylee met his gaze and her emotions collided into a blurted laugh before she stopped it.

Jamey's pinched lips and folded arms said he was less than amused. "I realize I'm not hulking huge, but I assure you, I'm perfectly capable."

Shaylee covered her mouth and shook her head, forcing away the smile. "Sorry, I wasn't thinking that. I just envisioned a poor hiker seeing you carry me through the woods. That might create some suspicion."

A slight grin tugged at Jamey's lips, softening his expression, and drew attention to the emerging goatee and firm jaw that gave him a rugged appearance.

Shaylee realized she'd stared a second too long when Jamey averted his blue eyes. "Actually, that's a good point. How did the guy get you up here, coffin and all, and bury you with no one noticing?"

The lightness of the moment vanished as Shaylee contemplated his words. The remote location and rocky territory didn't make for easy transport of an unconscious body. Not to mention burying a plexiglass coffin.

"Is there a path? Large enough for a UTV?"

Jamey nodded. "It's rough ground, but not impossible to traverse with the right equipment. He'd have had to come up the backside of the mountain. However, the roads are closed because of the sinkhole. Which means he's familiar with the area, too."

Baxter had the connections to do whatever he wanted. Shaylee studied Jamey. "How did you get up here?" A niggle of worry had her reassessing his help. Was he safe?

"It's a long story," he said, using her words. "My guess is your attacker had this planned for a while. Even dug the hole and placed the coffin inside before he brought you out here."

Shaylee moved to the boulder and dropped to a sit. The weight of the realization was overwhelming. Maybe she had more enemies than Baxter. Mama always said your enemies weren't the people you hated, it was the people who hated you. She'd worked many cases over the years, and criminals remembered who had put them away.

"That's a lot of premeditation," Jamey said, interrupting her thoughts. He released Bugsy's leash, allowing her to roam. The dog stayed nearby, nose constantly working the ground.

Fear snaked up Shaylee's spine. "Yeah."

Shaylee ignored the emotion, opting instead to lean into her insatiable curiosity. Her gaze traveled back to the coffin. The solid reminder of being trapped in the confined space, nearly suffocating to death, the cockroach that had skittered across her forehead, and the terror of her last conscious moments stole the breath from her lungs.

"Are you okay?" Jamey moved beside her, placing a comforting hand on her shoulder.

She nodded, not trusting her voice.

"How long were you in there?"

Shaylee shrugged and glanced down at the wrinkled clothes she'd worn the day before. Had she fallen asleep on the couch? Not unusual; she slept better on the sofa than she did in her own bed. But she had no recollection beyond sipping the tea in her kitchen. Had someone broken into her home and drugged her?

She ran her hands over her arms, looking for puncture wounds. Her hand went to her throat, sore from her screams and cries. How long had she been buried? Unable to speak, she walked away from the scene, desperate to put distance between her and the grave.

Jamey and Bugsy joined her, and the trio paused at the edge of the tree line.

Needing to ground herself and focus on getting to safety, she leaned down and petted the dog's short, soft fur. "Which direction?"

Jamey reattached Bugsy's leash, then snapped it to his belt. He withdrew a GPS device and gestured toward the right. "This way."

They continued through the forest in silence, each lost in their own thoughts. Birds chirped in the trees as if letting them know it was safe. Shaylee marveled at the ease with which Jamey and Bugsy communicated without words. The relationship spoke of trust and love. Two things Shaylee had forgotten existed.

Sunlight exploded as they entered a clearing, as though someone had opened the door to a cage.

Shaylee paused. Jamey turned to look at her. "Is something wrong?"

"Not at all." She inhaled deeply, filling her lungs with the fresh mountain air, and stretched her arms wide, embracing the openness. "Thank You, Lord." Her prayer came out louder than intended, but she didn't apologize. She was alive, and that was reason enough.

"Amen." Jamey and Bugsy stood at a distance, waiting for her to catch up.

She smiled and hurried to meet him. "I'm working on an attitude of gratitude, so whenever there's an opportunity, I just go with it."

"Great idea. Might have to try that myself." He withdrew his cell phone and searched again for a signal. "Still nothing."

"Believe it or not, the hike feels good on my back and legs. I'm walking out the cramps and tight muscles." Shaylee followed him. "How long can a person survive buried underground?"

He didn't immediately respond. Finally, he mumbled, "Nearly six feet by three feet, at a depth of—"

"Are you calculating?"

"Sorry, science brain kicked in. I'd guesstimate no more than two days, with access to oxygen, but I can't tell you for sure."

Anyone who had invested that much effort into her final resting place wouldn't stop until she was dead.

Jamey refrained from sharing his concerns that their shooter had mysteriously disappeared. Was he waiting for them somewhere on the trail? Or had he run off? He relied on Bugsy's calmness to measure their situation. Since she hadn't warned they were in danger, he focused on getting them to safety and cell reception.

Small talk wasn't Jamey's strong suit, but Shaylee had grown silent. "You okay back there?"

"Sorry. Lost in thought."

"You clammed up tighter than an *Armadillidium vulgare.*"

"An armadillo what?"

Jamey chuckled and slowed as they maneuvered around a tight bend, and made eye contact with Shaylee. "Fancy words for roly-poly bug."

She grinned. "Aren't you a wealth of knowledge?"

"Just about insects. They're fascinating." And the only topic Jamey felt comfortable discussing as small talk with a cop stranger.

"I can honestly say I have never thought of them as interesting. Although I remember playing with roly-polies as a kid."

Jamey took the lead again, his back to her. "Most people avoid insects, but they're amazing, like tiny detectives."

He clamped his mouth shut. *Stop rambling.* However, doing so might become problematic. The last thing he wanted to do was give her a peek into his twisted history.

Years of entomology education and forensic experience naturally bubbled to the surface. Jamey cherished study and investigation, relying totally on academic reasoning and his default ability to view the world through the lens of science. Even after Baxter had influenced Jamey's boss to fire him after the trial, no amount of time spent away from the discipline had diminished his love of science. Thus the career change to the high school science lab. Truthfully, though, Jamey still missed working cases. Entomology was like returning to a friend, and the only way Jamey made sense of the sadness he'd seen.

"I'm impressed. You're doing well considering you survived being buried alive just a little while ago," he said.

"I guess all those early-morning runs are paying off."

"Do you exercise every day?" Jamey probed against his brain's reminder to mind his own business. The sooner they got to a place with cell reception, the sooner he could call for help and they'd part ways. Whatever Shaylee was into, it was clearly dangerous. She needed armed professionals, not a washed-up forensic entomologist playing high school science teacher.

"Yes. Well, sort of," she continued, interrupting his reverie.

Any other questions he might have had about Shaylee remained unspoken. He didn't want to know. Ignorance was bliss, and as soon as they got her help, he'd go on about his life and pretend this whole bizarre nightmare had never occurred.

Whatever she wasn't telling him was more than he wanted to know.

He mentally congratulated himself on the self-control he'd exhibited by not pelting her with *why* questions. *Why* was his favorite word. However, he'd learned—painfully at times—that beyond the confines of a laboratory, asking questions tended to invade people's privacy. Shaylee's lack of communication burrowed into his core, bringing him to one conclusion: she had a secret. Whatever it was, that something or someone had almost killed him and Bugsy on the ridge.

What had he gotten himself into? His gaze traveled down the leash. Rather, what had Bugsy gotten them into? Oblivious to his contemplations, his bluetick coonhound trotted ahead without a care in the world.

Jamey's mind wandered back to the shooter, the camera

and the most disturbing object, the coffin. He'd testified as a forensic entomologist in a fair number of horrific cases. The clear plexiglass box was a new one in his experience. And the unsettling suspicion that the killer continued to watch them worried Jamey. He'd only worked on crimes after they had been committed, which was how he preferred it. Not that he'd ever testify or investigate again. He'd lost that privilege.

He focused on the path, overgrown in places due to the lack of use. They rounded another curve, and Jamey studied Shaylee. Her furrowed brows and the creases in her forehead said she was deep in thought. She wore black cargo pants and a lightweight gray athletic shirt, both smudged with dirt. Her wide hazel eyes and dark lashes held shadows of unspoken concerns. Everything about her awakened Jamey's senses with new and awkward feelings, in the best possible way, completely unnerving him.

He'd get Shaylee safely out of the forest and go back to his mission of finding Zia's body. Everything in Jamey's original assessment pointed to traces of gypsum, indicating Zia's remains were near the mineral. Regardless of Baxter's claims that Zia had mysteriously disappeared while driving home one night and his legal team's refutation of the prosecution's findings, the recent sinkholes revealed an underground gypsum mine. Jamey was certain the clue would lead him to Zia. However, the morning's events had added a substantial and attractive detour—Shaylee.

Yet, something in him like he'd never known needed to protect her, even if she wasn't aware of it or wanted his help. Except he was unsure who or what he was protecting Shaylee from. Most important, he returned to the biggest question. Why did he feel compelled to be the one to do the job?

He stifled a snort. Bug Dude, as his law enforcement

associates had dubbed him, didn't possess legendary defender techniques or even a gun.

"How much farther?"

Jamey glanced at his handheld GPS device. "We should come up to the bridge in a few minutes."

"Okay."

He scoured his mind for more conversation topics. Stumped, he remained silent.

What had she done, seen or been a part of that would make her the target of such intense hatred and maliciousness? His curiosity warred with rationale. Shaylee had no reason to trust him and, really, the less he knew the better.

Jamey spotted the bridge and exhaled relief. "We're almost there." A blue jay trilled from above, and the sound brought a smile to his lips. "Thank You, Lord," he whispered the prayer, imitating Shaylee's idea of exhibiting gratitude. Along with silent appreciation that the shooter hadn't returned.

She didn't respond.

He glanced over his shoulder to ensure she was following. Her eyes were downcast, and a frown marred her brows.

Bugsy slowed as they approached the bridge, glancing at Jamey again with wariness. "Come on, girl, it's just a weird sidewalk," he encouraged.

Undeterred and out of character, Bugsy sat planted in place.

"Is she always so stubborn?" Shaylee caught up to him.

"Not usually. She's smart and not a fan of bridges. We're still working on those and ladders. Dogs don't climb naturally—they have to be trained to do it. But the suspension bridge is a little different since it sways and makes her uneasy." Jamey didn't add that it hadn't taken this much encouragement to get Bugsy across the first time. Instead, he knelt beside his dog and rubbed her head and ears. "You can do this. You did it once already, so what's the holdup?"

Bugsy's dark eyes pleaded with him, and she let out a protesting woof.

Jamey laughed. "We'll discuss your opinions later. Right now, we need to get back to the pickup. Come on." He tugged on the leash, and Bugsy reluctantly followed.

"She might have a point. I'm not feeling super thrilled about walking across that, either. Is there another option?" Shaylee asked from the edge.

"Not without going around the mountain we just hiked. This area isn't open to the public, which your kidnapper must've known. Explains why he'd use it. No witnesses or people to worry about." Perhaps reminding Shaylee of the potential danger would help her join him.

"And you violated the law and traipsed over there, anyway?"

Jamey chuckled. "Well, when you put it that way, it sounds bad. Unfortunately, when we get called out to scenes, they aren't always easy to reach. Bugsy has to work in the environments without fear." And he completely danced around that topic.

"I guess that makes sense."

"Ready? Or do you want to continue procrastinating?" Jamey teased.

Shaylee grimaced. "That obvious?"

"Little bit."

"All right, let's do this. Onward."

Jamey and Bugsy led the way. The planks swayed gently as Shaylee stepped onto the bridge. They maneuvered their way slowly and steadily toward the center. He caught sight of Shaylee clinging to the rope rail.

A strange cracking halted Jamey. "Bugsy, stay."

"What's wrong?"

He listened again for the sound, gripping the leash tightly. "Did you hear that?"

Shaylee surveyed the area. Though the birds had stopped singing, nothing appeared out of order.

Jamey scanned the distance. Not far to go but moving faster would cause the bridge to sway more. Slow and steady was the key. "Maybe it was my brain rattling," he joked, then drew Bugsy closer, keeping the leash attached to his belt and reining her beside him. He gripped the handle on her vest and took another step.

A loud snap and the planks gave way.

Bugsy slipped through the hole, taking Jamey with her.

THREE

Shaylee sat with her legs outstretched, feet braced against what she prayed was a solid board. Her left hand gripped the side ropes comprising the handrail. She'd looped her right arm through the straps on Jamey's backpack. Heart thudding against her rib cage, Shaylee panted as she assessed the unbelievable moment. She'd reacted on impulse to help Jamey and Bugsy. Now she looked like a rag doll, clinging to objects in all directions.

Bugsy whined, desperate and scared, egging Shaylee into action.

A large portion of the backpack had snagged on a jagged piece of wood from under the bridge's floor and acted as a plug, keeping Jamey from falling through completely. Most of his upper half remained above the bridge, one arm holding on while his legs swung freely underneath. His other hand gripped the handle of Bugsy's halter. He claimed to have a tight hold on her, but Shaylee doubted he'd maintain the position for long.

Groans from the intact ropes gave a warning countdown.

"Take Bugsy!" Jamey cried.

"Okay, on the count of three, I'll let go of you and grab her halter." Shaylee leaned to peer under the bridge, causing it to sway slightly.

"Forget about me. Just make sure you have her."

"I need to readjust." She slid her arm free of Jamey's backpack and shifted to kneel, her hand still clinging to the side rail. Leaning down, she reached through the only available space to grasp Bugsy's halter. There wasn't enough room to lift her through the hole. "I can't pull her up with one hand. You're in the way."

Another groan from the ropes.

Shaylee spotted the last two strands straining to hold the bridge.

"Hang onto her." Jamey grasped the wood and pulled himself up, freeing his torso, then repositioned to a kneel beside Shaylee. Together they hoisted the terrified dog through the hole.

Jamey sat back, holding Bugsy against his chest, then slowly rose. "Go as fast as you can!"

Shaylee took the lead, and the three hurried off the bridge, lunging for the side they'd just hiked. They stepped on to the hard earth as the remaining ropes snapped free, and the rest of the platform collapsed into the cavernous depths below.

Two distinct sections of broken planks hung opposite the massive ravine. The boards swung freely above the jagged rocks.

Shaylee dropped to a squat, chest heaving from exertion and dread. Muscle fatigue shook her limbs. She sat and wrapped her arms around her knees, grounding herself as the adrenaline dump consumed her.

Jamey knelt, Bugsy pressed tightly against him. He buried his face in her neck. "Are you okay, girl? I'm so sorry."

The sight tore at Shaylee's heart. "Is she hurt?"

Jamey's fingers moved through the dog's short fur as he busied himself checking for injuries. "I can't believe it. There's not a scratch on her." He traced the long leash, still connected to his belt. "If I had failed to attach her to me..." He met Shaylee's gaze, fear swirling in his blue eyes.

Her stomach tightened at the horrible images and she shoved them down.

Bugsy wagged her bottom half while covering Jamey's face with licks.

"I'd say she's pretty grateful, too." Shaylee's attempt to smile fell with the guilt weighing her down.

Jamey embraced the dog, absorbing her affection. "Thank You, Lord."

Shaylee turned and studied the bridge. "There's no chance of us crossing now."

He stood and focused on the broken structure. "The shooter must've cut a portion of the rope and boards to make it break."

She visually followed where he pointed. "It looks old. Maybe the wood rotted?" Even as she spoke the words, instinct argued that wasn't the reason the bridge had come apart.

Jamey pinned her with a glare. "It was hardly rotten enough to fall through. Now is a good time to tell me why someone is out to kill us." Fury emblazoned his face.

She stood taller, nose to neck with Jamey. Her cheeks warmed with anger, and she opened her mouth to retaliate with a lashing of her own. A cold nose touched her hand, and she glanced down. Bugsy stared up at her, dark eyes full of compassion instantly undoing her defensiveness.

Throat tightening with emotion, Shaylee nodded. He was right. She'd endangered them by her presence. How many lives would she bear responsibility for?

They were innocent.

She wasn't.

Head hung, she focused on the ground and struggled to answer his questions. She was a human tornado of destruction.

"Detective Adler?"

Finding her voice, she explained, "I've put away a lot of bad people over the years, but my suspicion is Baxter Heathcote wants me dead."

Jamey gaped at her. "Baxter is, was, your brother-in-law. Why would he hurt you?"

A part of her reasoned she owed the stranger no explanation, but she couldn't deny that Jamey and Bugsy had saved her life.

Several times.

"I found—" She hesitated, biting her lip. Did she want to tell him about the journal? The fewer people who knew, the better. "Baxter is responsible for Zia's death, regardless of what the jury concluded."

"Your coworkers disagreed." Accusation hung in Jamey's tone.

"Baxter hasn't buffaloed everyone," Shaylee snapped.

Jamey harrumphed and crossed his arms over his chest in challenge. "So, what's changed? Have you found new evidence against him? What put you in his crosshairs?"

Shaylee turned her back to him. "I'm working on a lead."

"The case is reopened?"

"Not officially."

"And you think Baxter is determined to keep you from pursuing the lead?" Jamey asked.

"That's my guess."

"I hate to put a damper on your ambitions, but doesn't retrying Baxter fall into the double jeopardy category?"

Shaylee shrugged. "Since the prosecutor dismissed charges without prejudice, he can refile the case at a later date, but that's for the attorneys to fight about."

"True. And the court of public opinion is quite effective for an elected senator."

She liked the way Jamey thought. "Exactly. Baxter

doesn't deserve to be in office. One way or the other, I'm going to stop him."

"How is he aware you possess this information?"

Shaylee swallowed and faced Jamey. "I confronted him yesterday at his house."

He gave a low whistle. "That was brave."

Or incredibly stupid. "Clearly, he will stop at nothing until he shuts me up."

Jamey rubbed his neck, tension evident in his stiff posture. He emitted something resembling a growl.

"I don't blame you for being angry. Just point me in the right direction, and I'll make the trek alone."

Jamey shook his head and gestured at the path they'd hiked. "It's not like I can say, take a left at the next tree." His expression softened. "I'm sorry. I don't mean to be a jerk. I lost my cool at the thought of Bugsy getting hurt." At the mention of her name, the dog moved to his side and licked his hand. Jamey stroked her ears. "That's no excuse for my behavior, though. Please forgive me for the outburst."

No one had ever asked Shaylee for forgiveness. Unfamiliar emotions tugged at her heart, and she fidgeted with her hands, processing his words. He'd earned the right to be upset with her. He'd not signed up to be her protector or rescuer. The poor guy had been dragged into her living nightmare. "There's nothing to forgive." She cleared her throat. "I get it. Bugsy could've—"

"But she didn't." He put a hand on her arm, and she met his tender gaze. "Thank you for saving our lives."

Shaylee nodded, desperate to change the topic. "You said there's another way back to civilization?"

"Yes, but it's a brutal hike."

"Ready when you are."

"All right, then." Jamey reached into his pocket, and his eyes widened. He slapped at his jeans. "My phone!" He turned toward the bridge and groaned. "It must've fallen out."

Shaylee didn't speak. Now what? How would they call for help?

"Having communication with the outside world is too easy." His grumbled sarcasm accompanied the removal of his backpack to reach the handheld GPS. "We'll have to retrace part of our steps to get on the old trailhead on the other side of the mountain."

He clipped the device to his belt and removed a portable dog bowl. Using his water bottle, he filled the bowl and set it down for Bugsy, then withdrew granola bars and a second bottle for Shaylee. "A little fuel to keep you going."

She took the offerings gratefully. "You come prepared."

He grinned and averted his eyes.

Birds chirped overhead and sunlight warmed Shaylee's skin as she snarfed down the snack. Her stomach growled, reminding her she'd last eaten breakfast the day before. She needed the calories.

When Bugsy finished lapping up the water, Jamey shook out the bowl, folded it and slid it into the side pocket of the backpack. "Now, how about if we finish hiking? Together."

"I'd be grateful for the company."

Jamey knelt and checked Bugsy's leash, then studied the GPS again. "We'll go west. There should be an old path about five hundred feet from here."

"Lead the way."

"Are you sure you're okay?"

"Never better," Shaylee replied with what she hoped was a convincing smile and more enthusiasm than she felt. Her muscles were weak, but she wouldn't confess that. Not when they needed to get to safety. She'd soldier on. It was how she rolled. "After you."

Rocky undergrowth and uneven ground made the hike

challenging as Shaylee carefully searched for places to step. The events of the past twenty-four hours swirled through her mind. Frustration combined with anger propelled her with the energy needed to continue. Baxter Heathcote was sadly mistaken if he expected her to curl up and surrender to him. Not only would she find the evidence to charge him with Zia's murder, she'd add his attempted murder of Shaylee.

"You're one strong lady. I can't believe you held on to me." Jamey's compliment interrupted Shaylee's thoughts.

It took a minute for her to process his comment. "It's more about physics. I had leverage, you didn't."

"I've read stories of people gaining extraordinary abilities in a crisis and lifting cars off children. Kind of wild."

Bugsy and Jamey's near-death experience had spiked Shaylee's adrenaline, and the recollection twisted her stomach into knots. She shook off the horrid images of what could've been and sent a prayer of thanks again that it hadn't happened.

Still, uneasiness hovered like a cloud.

Would the killer believe they'd perished on the bridge, or continue coming for them? Or had he set up a camera there, too, and learned they'd escaped? What would they do if he returned before they got help?

Emotions were not Jamey's forte. His father had made sure of that, drilling endless reminders of how real men behaved since before Jamey could remember.

"Emotions are a sign of weakness, and weaklings get pummeled." Dad had emphasized the latter with beatings, ingraining the lessons and reminding Jamey of the damaged man he was.

Who was he kidding?

Nearly losing Bugsy had boiled his emotions to the surface so fast he couldn't stop them. So he'd lashed out at Shaylee. As if it was her fault some maniac was trying to kill her. Ugh.

She'd put a name on the killer: Baxter Heathcote. And Jamey wouldn't disagree. The man was capable of doing the unconscionable, despite the honorable image his campaign team painted.

Shaylee was hiding something, but his instincts said it wasn't malicious. Rather, it appeared she was a private person. As was he. Besides, he'd never leave her helpless and alone in the elements to die. Judgment didn't belong to him.

Jamey's neck and arms warmed under the sun, which was now high in the cloudless sky. He hadn't packed for an all-day adventure, and they'd need water and food. Based on the GPS and his calculations, thanks to the detour the destroyed bridge had created, they had a little more than a couple hours' hike to the trailhead, where he'd parked his truck. Barring any other broken bridges, gunfire or other assorted elements of death.

He'd have to return tomorrow to search for Zia.

"I'm floored at the beauty of those mountain ridges," Shaylee commented.

"They're called cathedral spires." Jamey pointed to the massive rock formations to the east.

"It's almost surreal. Do you come up here often?" Her cheeks blushed a soft shade of pink, amplifying her already attractive features. "Wow, that sounded super corny."

Jamey chuckled. "Yes and no. Bugsy and I work many areas. When school lets out for the summer break, we planned to do a lot of camping and Adam training."

"Who is Adam?"

He faced her. "The scent tracking device I train Bugsy with."

"You named it?"

"It's a human hand."

Shaylee shivered. "Ew. Can't you use a spray or something less gross?"

"It sounds bad, but decomp—"

"I get it." She lifted her palm to silence him.

"Anyway, I bury the item, and Bugsy searches for it." Jamey surveyed the mountain and sighed.

"Is that what you were doing up here in the first place?" She paused and looked around. "Wait, you said we're in Black Hills National Forest. Didn't they have some kind of sinkhole situation out here?"

Jamey hesitated. Now it was his turn to divert attention. "Yes."

"I need a little more information." She planted her hands on her hips, her jaw set in a stubborn line. She softened. "Oh, I wasn't even thinking. Are you here working on a rescue or recovery mission?"

"Something like that."

She looked around. "Where are the others?"

If he told her why he was there, she'd probably ask questions that would only ensure her disgust at him. She hadn't mentioned his testimony at the trial. Although once he elaborated, she'd piece it together. He rubbed his neck. Bugsy moved beside him. "I think the sinkhole may have revealed an overlooked crime scene."

Her eyes widened. "I'm not aware of any recent crime scenes."

Here we go. At least she was unarmed. "The sinkhole uncovered a gypsum mine."

Shaylee's hand flew to her mouth. "Gypsum! Like the traces you testified to on the bug things found in Baxter's trunk? You think Zia is buried there?"

He nodded. "We'll return to continue our search for it when we bring the cops to your crime scene. I hope to inspect the coffin, too. I must figure out what drew Bugsy there."

"But if the park is closed—" She blinked. "You're here of your own volition?"

Jamey swallowed. Would she be furious with him? He could dance around the subject, but her approval was irrelevant. Although if she arrested him, that would put a damper on his plans. Momentarily. Opting for the truth, he said, "Yes. I'd appreciate you not arresting me or throwing me into jail. I need to find her."

He waited, expecting her to explode or threaten him. Instead, she said softly, "Me, too."

Jamey continued walking. Neither spoke for several minutes.

"At least we don't have to worry about someone attempting to cross the bridge and contaminating the evidence," Shaylee teased.

"Good point." Jamey grinned.

"She was amazing."

He paused and turned to face Shaylee. "I didn't know her personally, but Zia deserves justice."

A quick nod and a shimmer in her eyes made Jamey want to pull her into his arms. Instead, he spun and blurted, "Tell me about yourself."

Why did his words come out like bad dialogue? *Ugh.* Although it wasn't the worst thing he could've said. He shifted into teacher mode. The past year at the high school had given him a unique ability to help students open up about themselves. Safer topics of discussion removed carefully guarded barriers, and people often shared more than they intended.

Whatever Shaylee had on Baxter, it was enough for the criminal to want her dead but not sufficient to justify an arrest. Yet. If she spoke about the case, she might accidentally divulge a little too much, and he'd listen for the clues. Finding Zia's remains in or near the gypsum mine and pinning Baxter for her death would reclaim Jamey's reputation. A twinge of guilt accompanied his mother's voice, reminding him that justified motives meant they were impure.

"—hiked for years," Shaylee said, reengaging Jamey in the conversation.

"Do you camp, too?"

"No. I'm more of a day trip kind of gal. I have a serious aversion to night-stalking creepy-crawly things. At least in the daylight I can see them and run. If I'm asleep in a tent…no way. No offense to your bug-loving self."

Jamey smiled. He liked her sense of humor. "Duly noted. I rarely meet anyone who enjoys the outdoors. I'd take being here over anywhere in the world."

"When Zia and I were younger, we'd babysit Noreen at her grandmother's cabin, near the Black Hills. We did mini hikes in the forest, but we never ventured far."

"Noreen Liddle?" Jamey clarified.

"Yes, our families are old friends."

Interesting. Baxter Heathcote's intern had been friends with Zia and Shaylee?

The path opened into a hillside with willowy grass and flowering plants.

"Absolutely gorgeous," Jamey said, focused on the lush green ground against the backdrop of blue sky and slate rock formations. He paused as two orange-and-black spotted butterflies flitted past. "Regal fritillary. Or *Speyeria idalia*." He gestured to the winged intruders. "They are striking nymphalid found among tall grass."

The leash grew taut, and Bugsy retraced her steps to him.

Shaylee drew closer, then bent slightly to see where Jamey pointed. The two butterflies fluttered around a purple wildflower. "I have no idea what you just said, but they're pretty."

"The one on the right is the male."

She leaned forward. "How can you tell?"

"He's smaller and has an outer band of orange spots."

"Maybe he's just underfed," Shaylee joked.

Jamey chuckled. "No, female regal fritillary are bigger."

The butterflies resumed flight. "Aha, see there? He's chasing her. The male always follows in a circular flying pattern."

"He's wooing her with his fancy aerial maneuvers." She smiled, and her hazel eyes appeared greener. The sunlight brought out red and caramel streaks in her raven hair.

"Breathtaking," Jamey whispered.

Shaylee stood upright. "Yes, truly beautiful."

He meant the company but bit back the confession. Averting his gaze, he turned and resumed the hike. "Sorry, didn't mean to slow down our trek."

"Are you always so in tune with nature?"

Actually, it was his one confident topic, provided no one forced him to testify regarding his observations. Grateful for the diversion and her obliviousness to his attraction, he replied, "As an outdoorsy person, it's important to be aware of your surroundings."

"If I have to learn all those fancy terms for bugs, I'm in trouble."

Jamey grinned. A third butterfly flitted past, searching for the sparse wildflowers. "Yellow Pieridae."

"Is that a secret code?"

He chuckled. "No, yellow butterfly."

"If I'm ever a game show contestant where I'm allowed to call for help about insects, you'll be the first on my list."

"Thanks. I think. I don't get many opportunities to impress anyone with my entomology skills outside of my high school science students." Jamey clamped his mouth shut and gave himself a mental slap upside the head. Why had he just said that?

"You sound like you really know your stuff."

There it was. Reminding him that she was fully aware of his failure at the trial and Baxter's legal team's perfect score at discrediting Jamey's evidence.

"—must have a very interesting life. A cadaver dog, teaching high school science and being a bug guy."

Jamey flinched at the nickname, then shook it off. "I'm boring to the hundredth degree."

They moved through a dense area. Thickets and underbrush covered the ground, and trees heavily laden with leaves overhead blocked the sunlight. Jamey searched for cleared areas to step. Even Bugsy stepped cautiously. "Be careful, it's a little overgrown here."

"Got it."

Their footsteps crunched on the sticks, rocks and twisted roots. It wasn't easy maneuvering through the thorny vines. Just as Jamey turned to check on Shaylee, she moved to the right and screamed, then did a strange hopping over bushes and ground.

"Shaylee! Wait!" Jamey hurried after her.

"Snake!" She fell forward, disappearing into the underbrush.

The slithering menace disappeared into a hole as Jamey and Bugsy reached Shaylee and halted. "Are you okay?"

She cried out, her hands wrapped around her calf. "It's caught!"

He looked down in horror. The steel jaws of an illegal animal trap held her foot.

FOUR

Shaylee relied on tactical breathing to fight the rising panic and the urge to yank her leg free from the trap. Images of the possible devastating injury she faced swirled. She knew nothing about such devices and no way of easing herself out now.

She'd never been squeamish, far from it, considering all she'd seen in her career. But experiencing—with full force—all her fears and worst-case scenarios overwhelmed her. Questions bombarded her faster than she could process them.

Would moving her leg worsen the injury?

How would she make it out of the mountains with an injury? She sucked in a breath, not daring to twitch an inch.

Would she die?

She struggled to comprehend Jamey's words over her roaring pulse in her ears. With both hands wrapped tightly around her calf, she glanced down and studied the vise, which was unlike anything she'd seen before. Expecting steel jaws to be embedded in her flesh, she was surprised to see her caged foot resting on a flat piece of metal. It didn't hurt as badly as it should.

She swallowed hard.

Maybe she had lost feeling because of the trauma. Had shock overtaken her body?

Thoughts raced. The most horrid and terrifying consequences had her brain circling the drain of possibilities:
Would she lose her foot? Bleed to death while Jamey ran
for help?

Why hadn't she looked where she was going? Easy
answer: she'd avoided the snake and hadn't considered
something worse might exist on the forest floor. The thick
underbrush had concealed the wretched device, not that
she'd have noticed it once she spotted the reptile slithering toward her. Without thinking, she'd bounded off in
frenzied flight.

Typical Shaylee response to go full force based on emotions and reap the consequences.

"Shaylee." Jamey touched her shoulder, and she startled,
glancing up where he stood over her. "I take it you haven't
heard a word I've said?"

"No, sorry."

"You're probably in shock. Keep still and let me look.
Don't move." Jamey knelt beside her and visually surveyed
the device, brows furrowed.

Bugsy inched closer.

Shaylee threw up her hands. "Bugsy, no! Stay back!"

The dog halted and tilted her head, locking gazes with
Shaylee in a way that conveyed confusion and concern.

"I'm sorry, sweetie. I just don't want you to get hurt."
Shaylee softened her voice.

"If it makes you feel better, it won't go off again." Jamey
gave her a small smile, no doubt meant to encourage her,
but fear was taking its toll and she ignored the gesture.
"I've got her. Sit, Bugsy." Jamey reined Bugsy in, keeping
her to his right, away from the trap. "Stay."

"Are you sure she'll obey?"

"She'd sit there for days if I asked her to." He stroked
Bugsy's ears. "Good girl." Returning his focus to Shaylee,
he said, "I need to move closer."

Shaylee nodded, then realized she still held her calf, prohibiting him from seeing the extent of the damage. She released her hold and leaned back, keeping her leg steady, allowing him a better view.

"Yep, that's what I thought. It's a bear trap."

"What kind of monster sets something so inhumane in a national park where a poor unsuspecting creature will get hurt?" Focusing her anger on the injustice helped Shaylee to suppress the panic attack threatening to explode.

"The unsuspecting creature part is the point of the trap." Jamey worked his jaw, clearly as annoyed as Shaylee.

"Why aren't they outlawed?"

"They are. It's illegal to hunt bears in South Dakota."

"If I get my hands on the person who set this—" She bit her lip to prevent the rest of the sentence from spilling out.

"Right there with you. The good news is, the trap's design holds the bear's leg rather than sever it."

Shaylee surmised that the pain suddenly coursing up from her ankle indicated her adrenaline levels were lowering. "How kind," she muttered sarcastically through clenched teeth.

He pushed back the tall grass, fully exposing the trap. "Can you wiggle your toes and move your foot?"

She blinked, aghast at the suggestion. "Won't that make it worse?"

"No. It's locked in place. I need to make sure you still have circulation and there's no tendon or muscle damage."

Shaylee refused to consider the significance of his words. She sucked in a breath. *Please Lord, let my leg be okay.* With tentative effort, she wiggled her toes and gently shifted her foot from left to right.

She exhaled relief, following it with a blurted prayer. "Thank You, Lord, for the pain in my ankle, and the ability to move my foot and toes."

"That's the first time I've heard someone thank God for pain." Jamey quirked an eyebrow.

She grinned. "Doesn't that prove I won't lose my foot?"

"I guess when you put it that way, yes."

Had she totally overdramatized the situation? Stupid emotions.

Jamey adjusted his position, moving opposite her with the trap between them. He gently shifted the device and revealed a short chain visible underneath.

"What's that for?" Shaylee gestured toward the silver link.

"The chain drags, leaving a trail for the hunter to follow."

"I'm disliking this guy more by the second."

"Agreed. Now let's get you out of that. Bend your leg slightly."

Shaylee did as he asked.

"See this?" Jamey crouched down and pointed to a piece of bent steel to the left, with a second section to the right of the jaws. "Each side is a spring. In the center is the pan where your foot is."

"As much as I appreciate you teaching Trap 101, could we do the lesson after my leg is free?"

Jamey grinned. "Nope, you need to know the terms so you'll follow my instructions."

"Okay." She studied the trap's design, noting the specifics Jamey provided.

"See how the sides resemble an alligator's open mouth?"

She nodded.

"Those are the jaws, and the arch they're connected to is the spring. I'm going to place my hands on the top of each of the jaws and force them down. When I do that, they will lower and relieve the pressure, allowing you to free your foot." His tone was calming, and his knowledge comforting.

"Wait, have you ever done this before?"

He met her gaze. "Do you really want to know the answer to that question?"

"No." She sucked in a breath. "Ready when you are." Her voice quivered despite her best acting efforts.

"Once the jaws are loose, slip your foot up and carefully out of the trap."

"Got it."

"On the count of three." Jamey counted and, on three, pushed down.

Shaylee freed her leg from the trap and scooted back.

Jamey slowly released the springs, and the trap closed. He lifted the ghastly device and turned it over. "There's no identifying information. We'll hand this over to the authorities." He glanced at Shaylee. "Or rather, you will." He placed the trap into his backpack. "Just to make sure no other unsuspecting innocent gets caught."

Gratitude flooded Shaylee. "You're a brilliant teacher."

His smile looked forced. Hadn't he said he was no longer an entomologist? He was clearly knowledgeable on so many things. Was this the same guy Baxter's attorney had pounced on at the trial?

Jamey's testimony had appeared indisputable until the defense expert tore it apart, making room for reasonable doubt, ultimately resulting in Baxter's case being tossed out. She struggled to reconcile the two Jameys. But proof was in the trap-releasing pudding, and Jamey had more than shown his capabilities.

Admiration for him conflicted with her doubts about him. "Thank you. You handled that like a pro."

He gave a one-shoulder shrug. "I had the simple task. Most people would've panicked. Your calmness made it go much easier."

If only he knew how terrified she'd been. But Shaylee shoved down the emotion, grateful she'd disguised her fear.

"Let's double-check your leg." Jamey sat beside her, reaching for her ankle.

"I'm fine."

She smoothed her pants and winced at the tenderness.

"I'm sure you are, but humor me. It comes with Trap 101." The corner of his lip lifted teasingly, and she relented.

His touch was like an electric shock, and she flinched. "Sorry. Still a little on edge."

He moved slower, pushing her cargo pants up to expose her tactical boots. "Would you mind removing your boot?"

She blinked, then nodded. "Right. Sure." Trepidation at his nearness sent Shaylee's heart racing. *Get a grip.* He was a professional performing first aid and nothing more. She untied and gently slid off the boot. Purple and blue marks had formed, and welts covered the flesh where the steel had caught her ankle. "I can't believe that nasty thing didn't break the skin."

"Your boots helped, but you'll probably have some mean bruises tomorrow."

"Considering the alternative, I'm not complaining. Thank you, Jamey." Out of habit, Shaylee stuck her foot into her boot, then winced at the tenderness. She yelped and Bugsy rushed to her side. "I'm okay, sweetie. Just need to slow down this time."

Bugsy sat and panted.

"If I didn't know better, I'd say she was smiling at me, except dogs don't smile. Do they?"

"Of course they do," Jamey said, getting to his knees and ruffling Bugsy's coat.

Shaylee pulled on the boot, then laced and tied it tightly to prevent swelling. She glanced up, meeting and holding Jamey's gaze. His eyes were dark like sapphires, encircled with a hint of gold.

She took his hand, and he helped her up. She wobbled

on her good foot, and he steadied her with hands around her waist. "I've got you."

His breath was so close she could feel it on her cheek. She allowed her gaze to travel the contours of his face, along the strength of his jaw.

Bugsy barked, gaining Shaylee's attention.

Jamey slid his hand to her forearm, and she stabilized herself. They stared at the forest behind them.

Bugsy lifted her nose, sniffing the air.

A whirring in the distance and a figure running into the tree line caught Shaylee's eye. "Jamey! Someone's out there!" She blinked, no longer able to see the person.

"Yeah, I saw him, too," Jamey said.

Just then, the horizon exploded into orange and red flames. Crackling consumed the air.

And then Shaylee smelled smoke. "He set the forest on fire!"

Jamey gripped Bugsy's leash. The gravity of their situation paralyzed his body while his mind raced in circles. A flock of birds overhead burst through the trees, signaling nature's warning to flee. Burning wood and embers blown by the breeze reached them. Like a starving beast, the fire was viciously consuming everything in its path.

And with each second, the danger drew closer.

There was no going back the way they'd come. Two viable options lay before them. Racing to the left would have them bordering the fire, but for a shorter distance. If they hurried, they might escape the mountain before the flames reached them. The other choice required them to hike an extensive distance over the mountain to the valley below. They'd have to follow the river to where he'd parked his pickup.

"What do we do?" Shaylee asked.

"Can you walk?"

"I'm fine." She waved him off.

"Okay. We need to move fast, but holler at me if it's too much." Jamey headed left.

Shaylee was at his side in seconds. Her gait was steady, but he caught glimpses of her wincing with her movements.

They walked without speaking, their footsteps crunching the pine needles and twigs dry from the recent droughts.

Kindling for the approaching flames.

Jamey allowed Bugsy to lead the way.

The heat intensified.

"We have to hurry," Jamey insisted.

"I'm trying, but how much faster can we go?" Shaylee huffed.

He glanced back. Her hobbling had increased. She was right. They weren't Sunday cruising, and short of throwing her over his shoulder, he couldn't do much to increase their pace. The crackle of the fire behind them worried him. The forest grew denser, foliage blocking the overhead sunlight. Jamey focused on the direction, ensuring they didn't get turned around.

Orange flames licked up trees. Too close. They were running out of time to reach the stream and cross over.

"We're almost there," Jamey said encouragingly, as much to himself as Shaylee.

"The fire is close."

They rounded the bend. A loud snap and two trees pummeled to the ground a few feet from where Jamey stood, blocking their path with flames stretching into the sky.

Shaylee grasped his arm. They stared in disbelief as the downed trees burned like logs in a fireplace.

Jamey spun. With no other option, they'd have to venture deeper into the woods and pray they found another clearing on the other side of the mountain. "Come on!"

He tugged Bugsy's leash and bolted into the thick tree

line, away from the fire. They maneuvered through the forest, their steps quick, breaths panting until they reached the edge of the cliff.

Glancing at the downward slope, Jamey scanned the area, mentally situating himself and estimating where the sinkholes began. He scoured the paths again, uncertain exactly which direction they'd need to run. With no other way out of the forest, they had to walk through the valley, leaving them exposed to the risk of encountering another sinkhole.

Unstable ground presented too many ugly possibilities, but staying on the mountains wasn't an option. They had to get to the clearing and find his truck.

Jamey surveyed the expansive landscape, rich with tree cover. How far away was the cordoned-off sinkhole? Traversing through uncharted territory had him a little turned around, but Shaylee's trust in him propelled him forward. He knew this land. They'd figure it out. Their lives depended on it.

"Jamey." Shaylee touched his arm, alarm in her eyes.

They'd have to make do. Certainly, they'd spot the caution tape preventing their entrance to the sinkhole. Or had the authorities only sectioned off the visible portion from the public road? They would not expect anyone to approach the sinkhole from this direction. More snapping and crashing of falling trees.

Smoke filled the air, burning his nose.

"Stay behind me." Jamey didn't wait for Shaylee's response. "Watch where you walk." The warning was overkill after all they'd experienced, but they couldn't risk another bear trap or snake. Precaution would save them time.

Together they barreled forward and downward through the trees, gravity assisting to increase their pace. Jamey kept Bugsy close, not wanting her to get hurt. The ground was rough, the untraveled areas harder to navigate with no good footing. He stumbled over rocks and branches but didn't dare stop moving.

The breeze morphed into wind, expediting the approaching flames. Ash floated around them, covering the sky in a hazy gray mist.

He rounded a curve, praying it led to a clearing. Relief collided with terror as the line of orange and red towered in an unbreachable force of fire ahead.

They were surrounded.

Jamey turned. "As much as I dread doing this, our option is to move in the direction of the sinkhole."

"I trust you."

Heat coursed from the flames, intensifying with every step. He refused to consider what would happen if they failed to reach safety soon. Jamey remained silent, unwilling to voice his concerns. Doing so enacted his worst fears and made them reality, solidifying their situation.

His gaze traveled the land, searching for the next safe direction. In the distance, he spotted a clearing. Thrilled at the promise of flatter ground, Jamey charged ahead.

He neared the bottom of the mountainous terrain and skidded to a stop. A large crack separating the earth gave him pause. Would he step into a sinkhole? He held out an arm, restricting Shaylee, and touched the ground with one foot, testing the stability. Nothing shifted.

Jamey leaped over the crack, Bugsy doing the same, and then he reached for Shaylee's hand to help her across. "Step wide."

They crossed the cracked earth and bolted forward. Relief that they'd avoided falling into the softer ground increased his confidence, and he moved faster. He must've miscalculated. They had more solid ground than he'd first thought. They rushed into the clearing.

Only a few more feet.

Jamey's foot shifted, and he felt the suction before he realized what had happened. In a gasp, the ground dissolved. His arms flew upward, hand still clinging to Bugsy's leash. Unable to stop the steep descent, he swung his hands wide, wildly grasping for something to hold on to.

His fingers grazed the earthen sides, and the walls gave way, crumbling through his fingers.

He plummeted in a free fall and landed with a hard thud onto the rocky floor below. His ankles burned. He pushed up to his feet just as Bugsy came hurtling through the same space and touched down with a yelp. Shaylee's scream reached him before she did; she tumbled into Jamey and sent him scrambling forward.

Crumbling noises above them had Jamey grabbing Shaylee and Bugsy. He tugged them away from the opening as the ceiling caved in, engulfing them in a cloud of dust and earth.

Bugsy sneezed and gave herself a thorough shake.

Jamey coughed to clear his throat, his hand covering his mouth. His eyes burned from the dirt mist.

"Are you okay?" Shaylee touched his arm.

He wheezed once more before replying, "I didn't expect that."

She looked around, then up. "Where are we? What is this?"

"My guess? This connects to the sinkhole I came here to look at."

The question in her eyes remained as Jamey focused on the situation. He removed his backpack and withdrew his flashlight.

Scattered grass, roots and twigs from the debris had collapsed behind them. The hole above was at least twenty feet high, impossible to reach.

He shifted the light, illuminating the walls of stone and dirt surrounding them.

"Can we climb out?" Shaylee moved to his side.

"I'm not sure how stable the edges are. We risk avalanching more ground and burying ourselves." He looked down and studied Bugsy, ensuring she hadn't injured herself in the fall. "Bugsy, you might be part cat. How many lives is that today?"

She wagged her tail and sneezed again.

The dry area indicated no water source. An opening off to the right was the only other way out. Jamey leaned in, and using the flashlight, peered as far as the beam allowed. "If this connects to the massive sinkhole, it will take us to the gypsum mine."

Shaylee seemed to study the tunnel behind him. "Um, but what if we crawl through that and it collapses and traps us?"

Potentially, and a scenario Jamey hoped wouldn't come to fruition. He turned again, studying the dirt tunnel. The larger sinkhole might have an opening where they could climb out. At least he prayed so. There were no other options.

"I wish I could offer a for-sure ending to this journey, but I can't. What I can tell you is that the mines are relatively stable, so if we find our way to that, we'll be doing good." And it would start with a leap, or rather a crawl of faith, right through the tunnel ahead. The space measured about three feet across and four feet high. They'd have to make the trek on their knees. "You're not claustrophobic, are you?"

"I might be when this is over."

Jamey grinned. Despite the horrible circumstances, he loved that Shaylee kept a sense of humor. "I'll go first."

"Put Bugsy between us. If something happens to you or to me, maybe she'll have a way out with the survivor." Shaylee's suggestion was thoughtful and sobering.

"Agreed." Jamey appreciated her concern for Bugsy's

welfare. But he refused to entertain any thoughts of either of them not surviving this adventure.

Failure wasn't an option.

Jamey slipped on his backpack, and with flashlight in hand, entered the tunnel on hands and knees. The hard earth and rock surrounding them grated on his skin. The beam illuminated a harsh and rough path ahead. The oxygen levels were lowering, making breathing more restrictive. His fingers grazed the bumpy stone walls. Clumsily he maneuvered below and above the long, serpentine tree roots intertwined along the way.

The intense darkness consumed the flashlight's meager beam, which did little to provide them a good glimpse into the next few hundred feet.

Jamey's knees burned with exertion. He really needed to exercise more. The rugged ground dug into his flesh under the jeans.

Bugsy whined.

"I know, girl, bear with me. We'll get out of this mess. I promise to grill you the biggest steak I can buy when we're done."

"Can I get in on that?" Shaylee called.

"Definitely."

The enclosure muffled their voices. The narrow passage prevented Jamey from twisting around to see behind him.

"Are we there yet?" Shaylee teased.

"I hope so."

But there was no way of knowing, and with each passing second, he wondered if they'd made a horrible mistake.

FIVE

If the tunnel collapsed, she would be buried alive. Again. Twice in one day would set some sort of record.

Irony at its best.

The flashlight beam bounced in Jamey's hand as he crawled, but the dim light provided only enough illumination for Shaylee to see Bugsy creeping on her haunches. At every juncture, the dog continued to amaze her.

Muscle fatigue shook Shaylee's arms and legs, and they burned with the exertion needed for her to keep crawling through the tunnel. Pain seared her ankle, squeezing the already tender place where the trap had clamped down. But she refused to complain. If Bugsy could make this trek, she could do it, too. Jamey remained silent, and Shaylee wasn't sure if that was a comfort or a concern. How far ahead could he see?

He slowed, and she paused. "What's wrong?"

"The tunnel narrows and curves."

"Is that bad?"

Jamey's hesitation sent Shaylee's heart into rapid rhythm. Were they trapped? "Your silence is very reassuring," she quipped, needing him to respond.

"Give me a second." He flattened onto his stomach and inched forward, crunching on the rocky ground. "Bugsy, stay."

The dog whimpered her protest but obediently remained in place.

Deafening quiet surrounded Shaylee, closing in the walls. Tight places had never bothered her in the past, but the lengthy confinement pelted her with uncertainty and desperation to escape the tunnel.

She swallowed.

The cold, stale atmosphere and lack of ventilation filled her nostrils with a mixture of dirt and dog, increasing her need for fresh air. Reminded of her time in the coffin, Shaylee suppressed the panic with prayer and practiced her combat breathing.

Jamey's departure with the flashlight plunged her and Bugsy into profound darkness. How long had he been gone?

Surely God hadn't brought her rescue in Jamey's arrival just to abandon them now? No. They'd get through this. *Lord, give me courage to persevere.*

Finally, boots scraped against the ground as Jamey returned feet first, the ambient light returning, as well. "I can't tell how far the tunnel goes, but I didn't want to continue without you guys."

She grinned at his confession. "No place to go but forward."

"That's my thought. Ready? Lie flat and army-crawl."

Great. Could Bugsy handle the long crawl? What if she panicked? Backing out would be treacherous. What other options did they have?

"Come on, Bugsy." At Jamey's command, the dog pressed on immediately, stunning Shaylee with her abilities and fortitude.

The rough terrain dug into the skin on Shaylee's palms, and she worried what it was doing to Bugsy. They moved on without speaking, the silence and dark closing in until Shaylee thought she'd scream from frustration.

At last, the tunnel opened. Jamey slid out, Bugsy behind him. Shaylee increased her pace, eager to be free of the confining space. She grasped hold of the tunnel's mouth, exposing her torso. Jamey and Bugsy stood in a wide cave. Relief overcame Shaylee as she took Jamey's outstretched hand and emerged from the tunnel.

Bugsy gave a thorough shake of her body.

"I hear that." Jamey chuckled.

"You're amazing," Shaylee said, praising the dog with a good back rub. Bugsy responded with a lick across her face and a rapid thump of the tail. "I thought that would never end."

"Me, too." Jamey shifted the light, illuminating the space.

Gray stone pillars supported the jaggedly cut ceiling, and boulders in varying sizes littered the uneven dirt floor.

"This is incredible," Shaylee breathed, wandering around the room. Her fingers grazed the walls where tool marks bore the evidence of mine workers. A chill swept over her, though sweat streaked her hairline and neck from the extensive trek through the tunnel. She plucked her shirt, airing her skin, and swiped her hair away from her face.

Darkness took on a whole new meaning inside the cave. With only Jamey's handheld flashlight, they surveyed the room, which measured roughly five feet by four feet. Interestingly, it was about the size of a county jail cell, Shaylee surmised.

She stood on tiptoe, stretching to her full five feet seven and three quarter inches, and grazed the ceiling with her fingertips.

"Have you recovered from the crawl?" Jamey asked.

"I'll have to recommend that workout to the instructor at the gym. I'm pretty sure I used muscles I didn't know I had." She rubbed her arms, working out the soreness. "I'm going to hurt tomorrow."

Tomorrow. The promise of another day and freedom infused her.

"They say the third day is always the worst."

"Aren't you a bundle of sunshine?"

He gave her a boyish side grin. "Sorry. I'll work on my presentation skills." Jamey swung the light along the room, revealing a second passageway. "Let's see where this leads."

They roamed through the space and ducked under the stone arch into a large walkway with a second stone pillar, supported by rotting wood beams that parted into two separate tunnels. The structure resembled eye sockets.

"Which one do we choose?" Shaylee asked, studying Bugsy as she investigated the ground with her nose. "Will she be able to find the way out?"

Jamey tilted his head, watching the dog. "We've never had an escape-from-the-gypsum-mine training, so your guess is as good as mine."

Shaylee grinned. "I appreciate our shared, dry sense of humor."

He chuckled. "Me, too, since not everyone gets my jokes. Although I suppose humor is a career coping mechansim for you."

"Naw, I've always been this way."

"Same here." Jamey lifted the light, scanning the rocky ceiling above.

"Are you certain this is a gypsum mine?"

He faced her. "The sinkholes exposed the mines from operations in the early 1900s. Until that happened, the authorities must've forgotten they existed."

Was it her imagination, or had he just diverted that question with a vague explanation? "But you're big into history and knew about them?"

He turned away and meandered through the area with a too-focused interest in their surroundings. He walked out, peering into each side of the optional tunnels. Definitely stalling. Why?

"Jamey, is something wrong?"

His shoulders slumped as though defeated, and he returned to her wearing an expression of resignation. "Our priority is to find a way out of here ASAP. If the fire consumes the area, it'll draw attention and beckon rescue crews. The bad news is, in the meantime, the devastation will continue tearing down trees and block our escape."

"I agree, but I get the feeling you're avoiding my question."

He gave a one-shoulder shrug. "I am. But let's talk while we search for a way out, okay?"

Shaylee surveyed the tunnels. Neither path looked especially inviting. "Lead on."

"I'm currently debating that. I'm not sure."

Bugsy maneuvered around the space, enjoying her freedom. Jamey left her unleashed and her steps quickened, heading toward the right tunnel.

"Looks like Bugsy says to go this way," he said.

"Well, then, I guess we follow."

They entered the narrow passageway.

"The structure is magnificent." The ground sloped and Shaylee pressed her fingers against the white stone walls bearing decades-old tool marks. She traced the engraved lines. Dirt mixed with red clay covered the floor embedded with rubble. A tower of rocks against one side had Shaylee wondering if they had avalanched at some point. She looked up, praying today wouldn't be the day the cave decided it had held itself up long enough and came tumbling down on them.

"I testified at Baxter's trial." Jamey's random comment echoed, regaining her attention.

Shaylee acclimated her brain to the discussion. "Yes." Why was he bringing up Baxter? Unwilling to dissuade Jamey from sharing whatever was on his mind, she remained quiet, allowing him to speak in his own time.

"Since Zia's your sister, I'm assuming you were present the entire time?"

"Every day." Like an old movie reel, Shaylee replayed the case in her mind.

Days of listening to Baxter's cronies drone on about his brilliant contribution to the community and extolling what a tower of strength he was to their state. Anger infused her afresh at the memories. Baxter's legal team had refuted all the evidence presented against him, explaining away the prosecutor's attempts to paint Baxter in his true light.

"Do you remember my testimony?"

Jamey's specific testimony wasn't at the surface of her memories. She did recall the moment the defense's bug expert—whom she'd disliked on sight—took the stand. A squatty man resembling a hairless chinchilla, and emanating deception with every word.

"Sort of," she confessed. "Something about insect parts found in Baxter's vehicle." She'd focused on the evidence hinging on his testimony, but the terms were all beyond her comprehension and the specific details eluded her.

Jamey paused and faced her, inhaling deeply. "I testified to the forensic evidence, specifically the traces of gypsum found in the trunk of Baxter's company SUV."

"That's right!" Shaylee mentally connected the dots. "You said the bugs proved Zia had been buried."

"In a roundabout way. I found a *Calliphoridae puparia* with traces of gypsum on the trunk carpet." He continued walking, moving faster, forcing her to hurry to keep up with him.

"Translation?"

"Blowfly cocoon casings. Blowflies are like the first

responders of the insect world after a death. They detect decay within a few minutes of a person dying. Anyway, without Zia's body, the prosecution had insufficient proof of her murder, or even that she'd died. The casings proved the flies existed on human remains and the gypsum provided significance to the location."

"Like this place?" Shaylee gestured toward the walls.

"Exactly."

"Please elaborate."

"Without getting all entomologist nerdy on you, basically it proved decomposition near gypsum. There aren't many places like that in South Dakota, a fact that gave Baxter's legal team their defense. At least there weren't before the sinkhole exposed the mines underground here."

Shaylee stopped. "So you came here looking for her?"

Jamey nodded. "My evaluation wasn't incorrect. Baxter is a murderer and needs to be held accountable."

Respect for Jamey flooded Shaylee's heart. She wanted to hug him for his tenaciousness in pinning Baxter, but doubt lingered in her mind. If they'd discredited his testimony once, how would he prove Baxter killed Zia? Would the prosecutor consider Jamey's new evidence? And worse, what if Jamey's assessment was inaccurate?

Faint whimpers echoed in the tunnel.

Bugsy halted, ears perked.

"Did you hear that?" Shaylee asked, unmoving.

"Yes."

She waited for him to explain. The sound filtered through again, eerie. A long wail that seemed to linger.

Jamey turned to Bugsy. "What do you hear, girl? Talk to me," he addressed her as though she'd launch into a full dissertation of her assessment. She tilted her head.

"You don't think the killer is down here with us, do you?" A chill snaked up Shaylee's spine.

"No. But we need to find the source of that noise. Bugsy, seek," Jamey instructed.

Bugsy barked, then hurried ahead.

"She's onto something."

They followed, forging through the underground labyrinth, dodging the low ceiling and clambering over rocky ground.

Though the dog never hesitated, Shaylee wondered if they were walking straight into danger.

The dark tunnel loomed ominous before them, and after all they'd endured, what waited ahead?

Jamey interpreted Bugsy's responses, and the urgency with which she powered ahead told him whatever she'd picked up on was important.

Had she found Zia's body?

What had made that noise?

All he'd wanted to do was get Shaylee to safety and now he was chasing his dog. Underground. While a fire raged above—courtesy of the killer—eliminating their chances of escape or rescue.

Everything Jamey hadn't planned on encountering today.

Would God help them? After all, Jamey had willfully disobeyed the authorities by entering the restricted park. Still, what were the odds of discovering Shaylee at that exact location and time? Surely God had brought him and Bugsy here for that purpose?

Lord, search my heart. I want to find Zia and get Shaylee to safety. Wasn't that the right thing to do? Weren't his motives altruistic? He didn't pursue fame or glory. Only the truth to be exposed.

He'd expected Shaylee to lash out at him when he'd mentioned the trial. Instead, she'd listened. Had she recalled the way Baxter's attorneys had attacked him, mocking his assessment? They'd torn him apart, making sport of everything Jamey held dear in the insect world. The memories ignited a fresh cinder of anger. Jamey might not be an expert in many topics, but insects were his specialty.

Had been his specialty.

All in the past, after his disastrous testimony.

Not only had Baxter's team painted him as an incompetent idiot, but Baxter had also taken special interest in destroying Jamey's career. He'd never been fired before from any job in his life. The memories ushered in the emotion afresh, forcing Jamey to remember his humiliating meeting with George Pritchard at his employment termination. He relived his fury at his boss's pathetic excuse after a decade of serving the department. They'd turned their backs on him. Even those he'd considered friends.

The desire to redeem his reputation had motivated Jamey to search for the truth. He might never work in forensics again, but being wrongly accused wasn't something he'd willingly stomach and ignore. And that was nothing to a killer walking free.

Bugsy's tail stood tall as she moved through the mine, drawn by some invisible line. The sound repeated, hollow and chilling. He didn't miss the way Shaylee favored her good leg. "Are you okay?"

"Yep."

He refrained from pressing her, but the wince on her face said otherwise. Shaylee seemed like the type of person who wouldn't confess her pain level, even if she was in agony.

As they walked deeper into the cavern, smaller rooms emerged, carved out of the stone. The ceiling also increased in height, and was now remarkably tall considering how far below ground they were. Jagged rocks poked up through the red clay floor, reminding him of adult teeth surfacing in an elementary-age child.

Bugsy ducked around a pillar, disappearing from sight.

"Bugsy!" Fear swarmed him. Where had she gone?

He rounded the corner and skidded to a halt.

Shaylee nearly ran into him. "What—?"

Bugsy stood protectively over a puppy, and the sound made sense. Whimpers.

Jamey inched closer. Dust covered the pup's black-and-white fur, dulling it to gray. A mixed breed, though she had border collie features. Probably less than twelve weeks old.

He approached with hand outstretched, squatting slowly. She cowered, dark eyes terrified and wide. "Hey, there. I won't hurt you. Ask Bugsy," he cooed.

The puppy lowered her head, shrinking back.

Palm up, Jamey allowed her to sniff him. After several seconds, her soft nose touched his skin. Too dry. "She's dehydrated."

"Poor baby. How did she end up down here?" Shaylee moved beside him.

"That's a good question." Jamey slowly removed his backpack and the portable bowl. Using his water bottle, he filled the bowl, then stepped back, giving the dogs room. The puppy watched Bugsy as she leaned in and lapped at the water. After a few seconds, the pup crept forward and drank vigorously.

"Aw, Bugsy is sharing with her," Shaylee commented.

"She's nurturing. I wonder how long the pup was down here. Looks like she hurt her paw. See how she keeps it lifted so it doesn't touch the ground?"

"Is it broken?"

"I'm not sure. Maybe sprained? I don't see any cuts, but it might have clotted with the dirt. Regardless, I don't have the materials or the training to fix her injuries here. I don't want to make them worse."

"You think she fell in here?"

"Or wandered in."

"Will she let us carry her?"

He reached out and gently lifted her, cradling the puppy securely against his chest while cautious not to crush her injured paw. "Looks like we're a go." Her downy fur tickled his neck and chin, and she trembled. "You're safe now, little one," he whispered, then glimpsed Shaylee watching him. His ears warmed.

"You're a natural with animals."

Jamey focused his attention on Bugsy. "Dogs aren't complicated. They're WYSIWYG," he said, using the acronym that sounded like *wizzy wig*.

"What you see is what you get," Shaylee interpreted.

"You continue to impress me."

She chuckled. "Law enforcement lives for acronyms. Where they don't already exist, we invent them. I assume by your comment you mean dogs aren't pretentious."

"Exactly. Their entire goal in life is to please us with pure hearts and no ulterior motives." Unlike nearly everyone he'd ever known.

Dad had always told him each person focused on taking care of number one. *Step on whoever you have to in order to get wherever you want.* That was Dad's philosophy. Even when it meant using his own family as a stepping-stone.

But that had never been Jamey's way.

He believed in justice. Doing the right thing, telling the truth. And as a result, Baxter had taken everything that mattered to him. Jamey's gaze traveled to Shaylee, and he averted his eyes. Were Shaylee and he on the same side? At one time he'd thought so, but he'd lost his career to badge-wearers like Shaylee. Authority figures willing to support a murderer with the power to influence their departments and the government.

Everyone out to protect their own jobs.

Out for number one.

Was Shaylee that way? Did it fly in the face of wanting to solve her sister's murder?

"Making yourself an enemy to Baxter won't help you climb the career ladder."

She snorted. "Believe me, I'm fully aware, and I don't care. Finding Zia and getting justice for her is all that matters. Whatever the cost. Do you have siblings?"

Great. Now he was going to have to talk about his own life. Which was something he had no desire at all to share with Shaylee. "We should keep moving." They proceeded through the passageway, and Jamey was grateful to have his back to her. "To answer your question, yes. Two brothers."

"Then surely you understand. Zia was my big sister."

"Were you close?"

An extended pause had him wondering if he'd said something wrong. Was she not comfortable talking about her relationship with Zia?

Finally, Shaylee said, "She was my only family."

"I'm sorry to hear that." The estrangement of Jamey's family had developed over the years. The chasm separating them grew wider with time. Not as though he wanted things to stay that way, but it just seemed no one was really interested in changing.

Shaylee continued, "How can I rest until Baxter is held accountable? I vowed a life of justice to speak for those who cannot speak for themselves."

"It's too bad your cohorts aren't as dedicated."

"Why would you say something like that?" Accusation tinged her tone and defensiveness rose in Jamey.

"Because they did nothing to support my testimony and the evidence against Baxter. He demanded my resignation. That whole standing-behind-you thing might work in your ranks, but not to the civilian staff who contribute to the process of law and order. They sold me out, probably afraid Baxter would come after them. Take care of number one, right?" Even as he said the dreaded words, he wanted to retract them.

Shaylee grasped his arm, and he stopped and faced her. "Look, I don't know what you experienced, or what happened after the trial, but not everyone fears Baxter, contrary to popular belief. Maybe your lack of evidence left an open door for them to refute your testimony. Isn't science foolproof?"

The words were a blow to his already bruised ego, welcoming the self-doubt he had befriended a long time ago. "Never mind, just drop it." He continued walking.

"If you gave them something to dispute, they found an opening and the case got thrown out. You can't blame the cops for your—"

Jamey's throat burned with anger and he spun around. "My what? Incompetence? Go ahead and say what you're thinking."

"I never said that."

She didn't have to. Because he'd heard it in his boss's pathetic justification for firing him.

He'd heard the words in the looks and actions of the jurors.

He'd heard it every day since the trial, every day he reported to work at his teaching job at the high school.

Jamey increased his pace, desperate to escape Shaylee and the cave.

SIX

Dissension as thick as Grandma's sausage gravy hung between Shaylee and Jamey. Once more her emotions had taken complete control of her mouth and she'd blurted things she couldn't unsay. Except, this time Shaylee wouldn't have retracted her statement, even given the opportunity.

Jamey's unfair perception of law enforcement and his dishonorable comment lumped her and Captain Dugan with deadbeats who bowed to Baxter's nefarious methods. She resented the implication, and Jamey's audacity infuriated her. Especially because he'd worked in forensics. They were on the same side. Couldn't he see that? The man's blatant animosity baffled Shaylee.

Obviously, they viewed things differently. How many times had she heard people blame cops for everything that went wrong? It got old. And she refused to believe her coworkers were shallow enough to cower under Baxter. Yes, he was intimidating, but just like Shaylee, those officers chose to serve on the side of justice. And justice didn't bend and bow to a bully like Baxter.

Or did it?

The thought poked her with a reminder that Baxter had, in fact, gotten away with murder.

And now she felt like such a jerk.

Because behind Jamey's anger, even in the dim light of the cave, she couldn't ignore the hurt that flashed in his eyes and lingered in his words. He said law enforcement officers had sold him out to save their own careers.

Like tiny Christmas bulbs on a tree, her brain lit up with understanding. He worked as a high school teacher. Had he lost his job because of the trial? The implication seemed ludicrous until Baxter's wealth and influence weighed against the rationalization.

The exhaustion and muscle fatigue she'd felt earlier transformed into adrenaline, fueling her steps. She needed more information, and that required talking to Jamey.

Curiosity at the development of the mine tunnels had questions bouncing all over Shaylee's mind. She bit back the inquiries, unwilling to speak to him about the matter at hand after their discussion. Neutral ground was the place to start.

She struggled to keep pace with Jamey's ridiculously long stride. Apparently, anger drove his movement, too, because she had to take three steps for each one of his.

Jamey turned, taking the light with him. Shaylee limp-jogged to catch up, refusing to admit her injured leg was delaying her.

She rounded the corner and nearly collided with Jamey.

"Didn't expect to see that." He gestured to an object suspended beside him.

Shaylee shifted closer and gasped. Sandwiched between a tall layer of rock and the mine ceiling sat an old car, circa 1950s. "How did a car get down here?"

He shifted the light and inspected the vehicle. "It's gotta be worth some money."

"Even crushed?"

Jamey faced her, and a corner of his lip lifted. "Hmm, good point. I should probably stick to my entomology expertise."

Shaylee smiled, the tension from their earlier dispute slowly dissipating. "Surely, it didn't plunge through the ground like we did. Someone drove it inside the tunnel, right?"

"Not necessarily. Flooding, other collapses, all kinds of factors could explain how this classic's life ended here. I'm hoping there's a large exit somewhere close where we can walk out."

"That would be a wonderful turn of events." She gazed into the long tunnel.

"We could try digging it out and driving it ourselves," he teased.

"And ruin this piece of history? Never." Her exterior guard of self-preservation melted. "Hey, what I said back there—"

Jamey lifted a hand, silencing her. "We're both tired, hungry and have been through the wringer. Let's just forget about it, okay?" But something in his eyes told Shaylee he wouldn't forget anything.

And why should he? She'd attacked him with her own assumptions. Whatever the reason for Jamey's attitude toward law enforcement, he cared enough about finding Zia that he'd risked hiking in a dangerous and prohibited location and saved Shaylee's life on numerous occasions. That alone spoke of his upstanding character. "Right. Sure." Her attempt at a casual response fell flat to her own ears, but Jamey didn't seem to notice.

"Although underground topography is dynamic," he continued talking as though they'd never skipped topics.

Shaylee glanced past him, where another tunnel stretched into ominous darkness. "Which way do we go?"

Jamey cast the beam in the space, unable to illuminate more than a few feet ahead of them. He stepped forward. "The temperature is warmer along here."

"Is there an opening?" Shaylee halted and Bugsy stayed with her.

"Maybe, it could also mean the fire is blocking that end, heating it up."

"Great." She swept loose hairs away from her face.

Jamey returned and knelt, stroking Bugsy's fur. "Well, girl, use your canine sense to determine which way we should go. We need to get out of here." He scratched under the dog's chin and met her eyes. "Bugsy, home."

Shaylee shook her head. Bugsy's abilities were nothing short of incredible, but finding their way out of the labyrinth seemed like a stretch. "You don't ask much, do you?" She extended her arms to emphasize her point.

"Never underestimate Bugsy. The command lets her know we're finished searching for the day." He snapped on Bugsy's leash and repeated, "Bugsy, home."

The dog's ears perked, and she sniffed along the Y in the path between the two tunnels, then took off through the second.

"Guess we're going this way," Jamey said.

They trailed behind her, the air growing warmer, infused with the scent of smoke and burned wood. The ground inclined sharply until they were practically crawling up the rocks.

A shard of light pierced the inky passageway. They continued toward it and paused beneath the opening above them.

"She did it!" Shaylee exclaimed.

"Good job!" Jamey praised Bugsy.

They stood under a gap in the earthen floor ceiling measuring two feet in diameter. "Looks a little small but I'm willing to risk it. We have an out, but how will we reach it?"

"Ladies first. Get on my shoulders and climb through.

I'll pass Bugsy to you. Grab the handle on her halter and haul her up."

"What about the puppy and you?" She hadn't meant to name the animal before Jamey, but he didn't seem bothered.

"Puppy will ride in the backpack." He lifted the little dog and spoke to her. "You'll be fine for a few minutes, I promise." Jamey addressed Shaylee, "I'll be able to reach and pull myself up, but I might need some help on your side." He was taller than her, so she agreed he had an advantage.

"Let's do this." She gently situated the pup in the backpack. "Hang on, sweetie, and we'll be done in a jiffy."

Jamey knelt on the rubble and stabilized his position. "Okay, ready."

Shaylee sat on his shoulders, teetering slightly. He wrapped his arms around her legs to steady her. Then, she shifted, and pressing her hands on his head, rose to stand on his shoulders, stretching to her full height. Her fingertips grasped the edge of the clay earth. "Go."

Jamey slowly stood, giving her better access to the rocky ground. With fingers clawing the dirt and foliage, she hoisted herself through the hole into blinding sunlight. Turning around, she squinted, struggling to focus as her vision adjusted to the change in light. Thick smoke burned her lungs, and she spotted orange flames in the not-too-far distance. She lay down on her stomach and reached through the opening. "The fire is making its way here. Hurry!"

"Ready for Bugsy?"

"Yes."

Jamey lifted the dog and Shaylee grasped her halter handle with one hand and braced the dog's belly with the other. She backed away, using her feet to dig into the earth in an awkward reverse army crawl until Bugsy appeared above ground. Once the dog's feet touched the soil, she reciprocated with wet kisses.

"You're welcome," Shaylee giggled and coughed. "Come on, Jamey!"

He was already making his way up. As his shoulders emerged through the space, Shaylee grasped the backpack straps, and working together, they freed him. As soon as he was on the other side, he took off the backpack and withdrew the puppy. She blinked rapidly, no doubt stunned by the bright sunlight, too. "Sorry, girl, but I didn't think you'd want to keep riding in the dark."

The pup's innocent and trustful gaze as she looked at Jamey melted Shaylee's heart straight into her boots.

A gust of wind blew smoke in their direction. Jamey pulled the neckline of his shirt up over his nose and Shaylee followed suit. "Hand me the puppy."

Jamey opened his mouth as if to argue, then gently passed her the animal. Shaylee tucked the puppy beneath her loose-fitting athletic shirt, protecting her from the smoke.

They stood and surveyed the grounds. Embers danced on the overhead mountain. The devastating sight tore at Shaylee. "So much damage," she said, before succumbing to a coughing fit.

Jamey leashed Bugsy and retrieved his handheld GPS. "Great news. I'm parked over that ridge, away from the fire."

Shaylee had never been more grateful for sunshine and open space in her life. They walked quickly, pausing only at an engine roar overhead. Mist from the rear of a plane sprayed the flames.

"Excellent, they've already got crews working," Jamey announced, shielding his eyes.

"I hope they get it under control soon."

"Do you think Baxter set the fire?" Jamey took the lead and Shaylee followed, eager to avoid traps and snakes.

"Whether by his own hand or he ordered it, I absolutely believe he's behind this. I can't picture Baxter chasing us around the woods, though. That would mess up his perfect appearance and dirty his expensive shoes." Baxter had no regard for life.

"Not to be argumentative, but that's extreme. And how would he get to us without Bugsy hearing him?"

"He wouldn't have to be super close to set the fire, and with the dryness we've experienced, it's as easy as setting kindling in the campfire."

"If you're right, and Baxter wants you dead, he'll go to any length to make that happen." Jamey paused and turned toward the mountain. "The fire destroyed the coffin."

Shaylee groaned. "I hadn't considered that. Of course, he'd eliminate the only evidence pinpointed at him. I wonder if the camera would survive since it's buried?"

"Well, there's always hope, but don't count on it."

"I should've grabbed it before we left."

"We preserved the crime scene," Jamey reminded. "Let's hinge on the killer's assumption his efforts worked. Thus far, we've experienced no further attempts on our lives. Although, I have to admit, I think he purposely pushed us toward the sinkholes."

"Why would he do that?"

"He'd assume we'd fall in and die, or the fire would trap us underground."

Shaylee considered Jamey's assessment as they started up the ridge. "We know the perp is comfortable and knowledgeable about this area. And there's a reasonable possibility he is still watching." A chill passed over her, regardless of the warm spring sun overhead and the burning forest behind her.

"Yeah, I've contemplated that not-so-great reality, too.

We need to get to a phone and safety as soon as possible. If he's a typical criminal, he's arrogant, assuming he eliminated us with the help of nature's elements."

Shaylee's boots crunched on the rocky terrain. "Except Baxter is incredibly intelligent. As much as I hate to admit that. And once we reappear in town, he'll resume his attempts on my life."

"Then we have to find the evidence to make sure he doesn't get another opportunity." Jamey's matter-of-fact announcement should've comforted her, but Shaylee couldn't help but focus on the enormity of the situation. Was this what Baxter had put her sister through before he killed her? If only Zia had come to Shaylee, she could've protected her.

They crested the ridge and Jamey lifted the handheld GPS, then gestured toward a path. "We're not far from my truck. Our perp did us a favor because we traveled underground in the exact direction we needed to go, away from the flames."

"Thank You, Lord," Shaylee whispered, cradling the puppy. Meeting his eyes, she said, "Just to clarify, I'm not thankful for the fire—it's horribly destructive. God provided a way of escape for us. But it's so awful to think about all those animals and trees annihilated because of one murderous criminal."

Guilt clung to her, unshakable, reminding Shaylee the damage was her fault. Once more, she'd been a conduit for the devastation of innocent lives. Ash blew in their direction, stinging her eyes. The smoke lessened slightly, but the stench of burned wood lingered.

Jamey touched her shoulder. "Fire also has healing benefits. Not that I'm approving or okay with what this jerk did today."

"How?" She searched his eyes, needing something positive.

"God has a way of using nature in amazing ways. The damage is significant, but even healthy forests contain decaying and dead plants. When they're burned up, they turn to ashes and the nutrients return to the soil instead of being held captive in the old vegetation."

She tilted her head, glancing at the area around them and noticing the lifeless places. "What an interesting perspective. Although it looks horrible right now, God will use it to regenerate the forest."

"Exactly. Like the scripture that talks about the Lord turning ashes into beauty."

"Isaiah 61:3," Shaylee agreed.

"Impressive. A woman who knows her Bible."

She chuckled. "My grandmother quoted that verse all the time." The levity evaporated at the painful memory forcing its way through her mind.

"You went quiet on me again. What's up?"

"Sorry, just remembering something I'd rather forget."

"You can't leave me hanging like that. Spill, Adler." He gave her a sideways grin. "I'm a great listener."

Shaylee sighed. "It's dumb. I got invited to the high school senior prom, which was a big deal considering I'd never gone on a date before. My folks didn't want to spend the money on a new dress, so they told me to wear one of Zia's. It didn't fit great, but we made it work. Anyway, while we were at the dance, I overheard my date talking to his friend. He confessed he'd only asked me out because he wanted to get close to Zia. I went home devastated, and my grandmother promised God would turn those ashes into beauty somehow."

Jamey had paused and faced her. "I'm so sorry."

She shrugged. "No biggie." Except it was. And why had she told him the painful secret? "I guess your teaching just gave the verse new meaning for me."

"You're welcome," he said with a grin. "Let's wrap up this hike. The end is near."

Gratitude for Jamey swelled her heart. Who was this man? He loved the Lord, was incredibly knowledgeable, and yet detested law enforcement. Her very identity. That would certainly be a problem in their relationship.

Shaylee stopped dead in her tracks. What was she thinking? They had a working partnership out in the wilderness. Nothing more. She nodded, agreeing with her internal evaluation, and continued walking. Jamey either didn't notice she'd held back, or gave her space.

"I just remembered another benefit of fires," he said when they entered a forested path.

Shaylee hurried to catch up to him. "Oh yeah?"

"The fire clears thick growth, so sunlight reaches the forest floor. It also destroys damage-inflicting disease and insects. And remember the butterflies?"

She smiled. "Yes."

"The wildflowers bloom again, providing them a habitat."

"So, after death new life begins."

"Exactly."

"God is too cool." Shaylee considered the way her heart had died in so many ways over her grief in losing Zia.

She'd given up on everything, including the good stuff. Friendships. Church. There'd been no romantic relationships to speak of before, and she didn't have the inclination for such time-draining activities. She hadn't walked away from God, but she had refused to participate in the church community. She'd disconnected, isolating herself.

Could her near-death experiences bring life to new beginnings? She hesitated at the edge of the clearing and traced a small purple flower with her fingertips. "I'm willing to try again, Lord."

"Yes!" Jamey patted her shoulder and pointed. "My truck is over that ridge, hidden in a grove of trees. We're almost home."

Jamey had never appreciated his Chevy Silverado pickup more in his life. He took good care of it, though a new paint job was in order based upon the pockmarked side panels. But the truck's tires were solid, and he preferred the manual transmission. Most important, he didn't owe anything on the reliable vehicle. Seeing the block of steel was like returning to an old friend, and the thousand pounds he'd borne throughout the day slid off as he hurried forward. Bugsy joined his enthusiasm and tugged hard on her leash. "I'm coming," he laughed.

"If I didn't know better, I'd say you two wanted to get out of here," Shaylee teased.

"You got that right."

Soot dusted the truck but thankfully the fire hadn't reached the valley or neared the ridge enough to do harm to it. Jamey unlocked the doors using his key fob, and opened the passenger door. Shaylee settled into the seat with the puppy securely in her lap. He loaded Bugsy into the back seat and slid behind the wheel. The engine coming to life sounded as joyful as the "Hallelujah Chorus."

"Yay, God! I could get used to this gratitude thing you do," he explained to Shaylee.

She chuckled. "I can name worse habits."

"Absolutely." Jamey shifted into Reverse. "I had to take a back road, which requires driving in a big loop, but we should be out of the traffic for the fire crews since they'll go up the main highway."

"Will it be closed because of the fire?"

"It's a neglected, single-lane, minimum-maintenance road, so I don't think so."

"I didn't realize manual trucks even existed anymore. I learned to drive on a clutch."

"Me, too. This pickup and I have been through a lot together. She still runs and I actually like the manual better. Makes me feel like I have more control over the vehicle." He pulled onto the road. "Where to first? The police department?"

"No, my house. I'll call my boss from there."

Jamey must've exhaled his relief a little too loudly, because Shaylee turned to look at him. "I'm so grateful you said that. I'd prefer to avoid walking through the PD," he explained.

"I'm hoping you'll allow me to change your opinion."

Jamey worked his jaw, contemplating his rationalized response. He owed her a reason for why he held such an opposing attitude. "For the record, I'm not against everyone in law enforcement. I appreciate what you do for the sake of your job and the public's safety. I believe in taking down bad guys to protect our communities."

"Okay…"

"It's complicated."

"I'm listening."

Would Shaylee bite his head off when he told her? They'd finally gotten to a place where their conversation was comfortable again. He sighed. *Spill it. She already knows about the trial.* "I support upholding the law, but all those involved in Baxter's case made me a joke."

"How?"

"Science isn't like people see on TV. There's no forty-five-minute investigation with jaw-dropping tantalizing testimonies and a slam dunk where the scientist comes in and produces evidence with a super cool explanation. In truth, science is a part of the whole and it's very rare that one piece of evidence alone solves the case."

"True. But yours was a portion."

"Exactly. The only *scientific* portion. Without a body, the prosecution already had an uphill battle with Zia's case." Much like the treacherous mountain road Jamey drove on at the moment.

"Her car was discovered parked at the lake, but without evidence of foul play, all that did was provide reasonable doubt. Regardless of Baxter's ludicrous claims, Zia would never have just walked away from her life or from me. Her bank account and credit cards weren't even used after her disappearance," Shaylee added.

Jamey nodded, remembering the details from the case. "The *puparia* I found proved there had been human remains in the trunk but didn't specify whose. And when Baxter's legal team pounced on it with that…that…" He searched for words to describe their expert. "Anyway, their refutation was that anybody could've driven the SUV. Once their expert finished his assessment, he baffled the jury with a convoluted explanation. Basically, they buried 'Bug Dude's' testimony by confusing the jury." *Bug Dude.* That was what they'd called Jamey. "It's my pride that's wounded. Plain and simple."

Shaylee was a welcomed member of the blue brotherhood. She would never understand what it felt like to be on the outside of the organization that relied on your advice, then trashed you with ridicule the next minute. He'd trusted them, sacrificed his personal life by putting the job first, and worked his hardest on the combined mission to put away bad guys. And when he'd needed their support, they'd abandoned him.

"So the prosecution hinged all their hopes on your testimony, and when it didn't go as planned, they tossed Bug Dude out with the bathwater?" Shaylee asked. "No wonder you're bitter."

"I wouldn't say I'm bitter per se," he grunted. "Ugh.

Fine. Yes, I guess I am. Thing is, I loved being an ento-mologist. Baxter destroyed that."

"I can't imagine losing my career. It's all I know. I've made it my life."

"Same here. Well. Had."

"Seems to me the prosecutor should have had more ev-idence than the insect casings. But we'd hoped the little they had would be enough."

"They had some, mainly circumstantial, though. And contrary to popular belief, you can have a case based on circumstantial evidence, but there has to be a lot of it."

"I'm sorry they treated you badly."

The words were a strange balm to his heart. Was it possible his own perception was clouding his judgment? Maybe he wasn't the biggest joke in the department. He could only hope. "Well, once I find Zia's body, I'll have the evidence against Baxter. He won't be able to squirm and slither out of it with his lies and money."

"Nothing would make me happier."

They drove in silence and he downshifted to gain torque to climb the mountain. The engine growled with deter-mination as they crested the hill, and gravity assisted in their descent down the other side. They picked up speed. He pushed in the clutch and tapped the brakes, but the truck didn't slow.

He tried again.

Nothing.

"What's wrong?"

"I don't know." Attempting to reduce his speed, he again pressed the pedal to the floor.

The truck accelerated.

"Jamey."

He shifted into Neutral, foot slamming the brake against the floorboards several more times.

They barreled on.

The curving topography became more treacherous and dangerous. He gripped the steering wheel tighter. Centrifugal force shoved them to the left and right as he maneuvered the narrow, single-lane road. In order to make the next corner, Jamey had to go wide, taking the apex in the center of the road to keep the truck on all four tires.

"Jamey!" Shaylee cried again.

"I don't have any brakes!"

He searched ahead for anything to slow them. The road flattened and a large open field filled with wildflowers and bushes came into view. Jamey downshifted, the truck growling in protest from the high speed that conflicted with the lower gears.

They slowed, yet moved too fast for the turn he'd need to make.

He again downshifted.

The engine gave a low rumble and continued slowing.

Still too fast, but better. If he could pull off into the field, he'd have dirt and plants to help reduce their speed.

"Make sure your seat belt is tight and you have hold of the puppy." Jamey glanced in the rearview mirror, catching sight of Bugsy. If he hit anything, she might be hurt. "Pray like you've never prayed before."

Shaylee's petitions filled the cab while Jamey's mind agreed with her pleas. He spotted the wide span of bushes. Better than a tree. And hopefully as strong. Again, he downshifted, now in second gear. The truck's speed had decreased, but not enough to stop without rolling the vehicle.

"Lord, guide us, please," he pleaded, jerking the wheel. The force sent him leaning hard against the door. They bounced across the ground, dirt and rocks slamming the underside of the truck. He aimed for the long row of brambles and bushes, praying the foliage would slow them down before they reached the tree line.

He lowered into first gear, worried he'd destroy the transmission, or worse, they wouldn't stop. The truck whined against the high RPMs, fighting the slower speed. He prepared to blow the engine.

The approaching trees grew bigger, closer with each second.

"Bugsy, floor!" he ordered. "Brace, Shaylee!"

With a slam, they rumbled through the prairie land and over the bushes. His truck pressed through like a stubborn bull forcing its way through a wall. The tree line posed a potentially unpleasant resolution.

"Please stop. Please," Jamey whispered. He squeezed his eyes shut, prepared to hit the trees.

But the resistance helped, and finally, the vehicle stopped.

Jamey opened his eyes in disbelief at the tree trunk kissing the edge of his hood. He quickly killed the engine and leaned his head against the steering wheel, silently praising God for the amazing rescue.

He spun around, ensuring Bugsy was okay. She sat on the floorboard of the back seat, looking up at him. Tail thumping.

Jerking to look at Shaylee, he asked, "Is there any danger we haven't faced today?"

SEVEN

Shaylee blinked, one hand braced against the dashboard, the other protecting the puppy. She stared in disbelief at the tree trunk just inches from the pickup's hood.

"Are you okay?" Jamey's voice registered, drawing her attention.

Unable to speak, she nodded, prying free her claw hold on the truck. She scooted back in the seat, withdrawing her hand from the puppy, who appeared oblivious to the brush with death.

"She's content. Great job shielding her."

Shaylee glanced down and stroked the sleeping animal. "You should teach emergency driving. That was pretty impressive. Is Bugsy okay?"

Jamey leaned over the seat and glanced behind them. "Yep, she stayed down on the floorboards. I'm grateful we had a manual transmission. Otherwise, I'm not sure that would've ended so well. I need to see the extent of the damage." He opened his door and slid out.

Shaylee's heart drummed hard against her chest, and her pulse pounded in her throat.

She pushed open her door and joined Jamey, walking the perimeter of the truck.

"How did the killer know where I'd parked my vehicle?"

The pickup was an older model, but Jamey clearly took

good care of it. "No offense, but is there any chance the brakes were bad?"

He jerked to look at her. "No. There's not." There wasn't a hint of reservation in his tone.

"Dumb question."

"Any other day, it would be a possibility."

"Right." Shaylee faced the road. "On a positive note, you were right about no one traveling around here. At least we didn't pass any other vehicles."

"Yeah, except now we're going to have to hike across the valley to the nearest road to get a ride."

"Easy peasy after all we've endured."

"I love your optimism." Jamey released Bugsy from the back seat. "If nothing else, maybe they'll allow me to borrow a cell phone to call a tow truck."

"I'm not sure it's safe for us to hang out here and wait, though."

"I agree."

Shaylee reached inside for the puppy. In her peripheral vision, Jamey removed his backpack and locked the vehicle. The tall grass swayed around her calves, and she scanned the ground before stepping, not wanting a repeat of the mountain dangers.

Jamey joined her, and they crossed the valley, finally reaching the road, empty of passersby.

They perched on a fence and watched for approaching vehicles.

"Where's a good traffic jam when you need one?" Shaylee quipped.

"Murphy's Law."

"Always a crowd favorite."

He groaned. "If you'll keep the dogs, I'll wave down the first vehicle we see."

"Got it." She took the leash from Jamey, and Bugsy dropped to sit beside her.

Jamey paced the road, using binoculars from his backpack. "Finally," he mumbled.

Shaylee spotted the maroon minivan approaching from the oncoming lane as Jamey stepped out, keeping close to the shoulder, and waved his arms to attract the driver.

The minivan slowed, and he hurried to it. After all they'd endured, Shaylee committed the out-of-state plates to memory in case they needed to report another attempt on their lives. Unable to hear Jamey from where she stood, she watched intently as he spoke to the driver while pointing to her and the dogs.

After several seconds, he returned to her. "Daryl and his wife, Tara, have offered to give us a ride to town."

Once more Jamey astounded her with his effortless ability to talk to people. "Outstanding."

He took Bugsy's leash and Shaylee followed him to the minivan.

Both side doors opened simultaneously, and the driver stepped out. "Daryl Moorhouse."

He extended a hand to Shaylee, and she returned the gesture. "Shaylee Adler."

"Sorry y'all had some car trouble." Daryl looked to be in his twenties. He had a shock of curly red hair and kind brown eyes.

Shaylee nodded. "Yes, but thanks to Jamey's skilled driving, we lived to tell the tale."

"Hop in. I hope you don't mind riding in the back. Tara gets carsick now that she's pregnant." He gestured at the attractive brunette in the passenger seat, who was smiling and rubbing her ample belly.

Shaylee grinned and climbed inside the van. "Not at all. Thank you for stopping and helping us."

Bugsy scooted beside her, and Jamey dropped onto the seat behind Tara.

"I'm Shaylee."

"Nice to meet you." The woman twisted around in her seat as much as her condition allowed. "My sweet hubby's always on the lookout to help people." She glanced at Daryl with adoring eyes.

They were too cute, and Shaylee couldn't help the twinge of longing in her own heart. Would she ever share a love like that with a man?

"Thanks again for the ride," Jamey said.

"A puppy!" Tara exclaimed.

"We found her. Poor darling has an injured paw," Shaylee explained, holding the pup a little higher for Tara to see.

Tara frowned. "Who would leave an innocent baby out there alone?" She reached over to stroke the puppy's head. "I'm so glad she found you."

"Me, too." Shaylee glanced at Jamey and he winked.

Daryl shifted into Drive. "Where did you need to go?"

"Black Hills Police Department," Shaylee said.

Jamey shot her a look, apparently irritated with her change of mind.

She shrugged. No point in dancing around it. They needed to report everything. Now. His ego or fears would have to take a rest.

Conversation was easy with Tara and Daryl, making the ride quick. The Nebraska couple had traveled to South Dakota for one last vacation before their first child, a boy named Daryl Jr., entered the world. The couple talked over one another, conveniently helping Shaylee and Jamey to keep the focus off themselves.

Shaylee told Tara about some of the best tourist sights while Jamey shared the national park treasures. Daryl pulled up to the PD and turned to face them. "Would you like us to wait?"

"No, thanks. We'll be able to borrow a vehicle."

Daryl quirked a brow. "They do that here?"

Shaylee chuckled. "Only for officers." She'd refrained

from telling him she was a detective, but no longer felt the need to conceal that detail.

A knowing smile covered Daryl's face. "Well, ma'am, thank you for your service to the community."

"My pleasure," Shaylee acknowledged as she climbed out of the van with the puppy cradled against her chest. Jamey and Bugsy got out, as well.

Tara waved as they drove away.

"Could those two be any cuter?" Shaylee smiled.

"Aw, yes, young love. Why didn't you tell him you were an officer initially?" Jamey asked.

"Not everyone is receptive to cops," she replied, averting her eyes.

"Right. Hey, while you talk to your boss, I'll go on over there and call a tow truck." He pointed to the diner across the street.

"Oh, no, you don't. I need you to explain to Captain Dugan everything up to the point where you found me."

Jamey groaned. "Fine."

They entered the front doors, and Shaylee waved to Franny, the receptionist. She held the phone receiver against her ear and responded with a roll of her eyes and a mocking gesture with one hand, indicating the caller was talkative. Shaylee grinned and led Jamey toward Captain Dugan's office.

She rapped twice on the opened door. "Sir?"

Dugan glanced up at her. "'Bout time you got here. I've been calling you all morning." He glanced over her shoulder and spotted Jamey. "Sir, I'm going to have to ask you to wait outside for just a moment."

What was up with Dugan? Shaylee motioned for Jamey to follow her to an empty office. She pointed to the phone on the desk. "Not sure what that's about but go ahead and call the tow truck. No matter what you hear coming from his office, ignore it. I'll be right back." She passed him the puppy.

Jamey shot her a worried glance, and she gave him a small smile of reassurance, then returned to Captain Dugan's office to take her beating.

"Close the door."

Shaylee did as ordered, then dropped into a chair opposite his desk. "Sir, before you say anything—"

"Not a word, Detective. Just listen."

Dugan was in a mood. Shaylee clamped her mouth shut.

The captain folded his hands on his desk and scooted forward. "First of all. We give you a department-issue phone with the expectation you answer it when I call you."

"I wasn't—"

"Just listen!"

Shaylee swallowed.

"You threatened to kill Senator Heathcote?"

She hesitated and processed Dugan's question.

"Answer me, Detective."

Recalling the incident with Baxter Heathcote, she cringed. "Technically, I said life as he knew it was about to end. Meaning his freedom. And with all due respect, he hasn't been sworn in yet, which is why I had to expedite questioning him."

Dugan grunted and mumbled something unintelligible. "Let's try this again. Detective Adler, did we or did we not agree you were to consult me before contacting or confronting *Senator-elect* Baxter Heathcote?" He exaggerated the title, enunciating each word, Dugan's classic controlling-his-mood move.

She didn't dismiss his effort or take it lightly, considering his department-legendary temper of which she was fully aware, having set the man off on more than one occasion.

Dugan shoved back his chair and stood, then squared

himself to his full five-foot-four-inch stature. His bald head had turned beet red, and the big vein pulsated on his forehead.

Her brain detoured, temporarily disconnecting from her mouth, and she blurted, "There wasn't time. I found a copy of an accounting journal in Zia's Bible. It's proof Heathcote doctored his finances—"

"—evidence he's accepting bribes?"

"Well, no."

"Shows he is keeping two sets of books? He's using a fake company to funnel money to an offshore account?"

Shaylee studied her fingers. "It's a ripped page from a book."

"Tell me you have the majority of the incriminating document."

Unwilling to disclose her uncertainty about what she had found the night before, she hesitated before responding, "Sir, that's why I needed to talk to him. To get him to confess the truth about it."

Dugan moved around his desk and paced the length of the room. "Let me get this straight. You stormed, unannounced and uninvited, into Baxter Heathcote's house, during a dinner party full of guests and witnesses, fully loaded for war, with the expectation he'd drop to his knees and confess to murdering your sister based on a ripped piece of paper?" With each word, Dugan's voice increased a decibel.

When he broke it down like that, her actions appeared rookie-foolish. Shaylee held her tongue, wanting desperately to crawl under a rock. She glanced at the door, wondering how much Jamey overheard.

Dugan sighed, then returned to his desk and perched on the end. "I know you loved Zia, and Heathcote is guilty. But he got away because of the lack of solid evidence implicating him specifically. He won't confess to anything.

Most especially not to murdering his wife." His fatherly tone replaced his frustration.

Shaylee wanted to argue, but Dugan was right. She sighed. "I'm sorry. That wasn't smart." How could she explain the emotions that raged through her at finding the first tangible evidence of Heathcote's criminal activity? If only she understood what it meant.

"Adler, you must talk to me before you go off next time. We'll formulate a plan together. Heathcote's got long arms and deep pockets. We have to be wise as serpents and gentle as doves, remember?" He referenced one of Shaylee's favorite scriptures and she smiled.

"Roger that. Now that I've taken my beating, can I tell you why I'm here on a Saturday morning?"

Dugan quirked an eyebrow. "I assumed you came here because of my phone message." He seemed to study her. "Although you look a little ruffled, kiddo. What'd I miss?"

Shaylee moved to the edge of her seat. "The man out there waiting to come in is Jamey Dyer." She paused for Dugan to process the name.

A few seconds ticked by and his eyebrows peaked. "The forensic entomologist?"

"One and the same. And you're never going to believe how I ran into him. Before I continue, I've not shared any information about the journal with him."

"Besides everyone within earshot of your tirade at Heathcote's house," Dugan retorted.

Shaylee cringed. "Right."

"Okay. So why not tell Dyer?"

"I didn't want to endanger his life."

Dugan quirked an eyebrow.

"I promise, once we explain the whole story, it'll all make sense."

"Bring him in. I can't wait to hear this."

* * *

"Mr. Dyer, Shaylee tells me you two have quite the tale to share. I'm Captain Dugan," he announced as if Jamey hadn't read the words on the door.

Bugsy sat at Jamey's feet, ears perked and pensive, in tune with Jamey's unease. "Yes sir, and this is my dog, Bugsy."

"I remember you from Heathcote's trial."

Jamey swallowed. *Of course you do.*

Shaylee caressed the puppy sleeping contently on her lap and perched on the end of her seat. "Last night, I was on my couch sipping chamomile tea. The next thing I know, I'm buried alive in a clear coffin. Coyotes scratched the dirt from the surface, exposing the lid, and woke me."

Dugan's eyebrows rose and his face flushed pale, his concern as telling as a news report.

Jamey listened as Shaylee recounted the events with calmness and composure. A shiver went through him at the thought of the moments of sheer terror she would've experienced before he arrived.

"I must've passed out again, because when I came to, Jamey had freed me." Shaylee nodded at him. "He and Bugsy saved my life."

"We need to have you see a doctor. Make sure you're okay."

"I'm fine, sir. Really."

Dugan addressed Jamey, and his eyes narrowed. "I owe you a huge debt of gratitude for rescuing Adler. I'm curious, though. How did you find her in the mountains? You just happened to come across her?" Suspicion dripped from his tone.

Jamey's shoulders stiffened, and he shoved down the rising defensiveness. It wasn't an unreasonable question. "Actually, Bugsy and I were—" he hesitated "—working in the area when she indicated on the disturbed dirt. Bugsy located Shaylee."

"She's search and rescue trained?"

"Yes, but we weren't functioning in that capacity at the time." Jamey squared his shoulders, prepared for the consequences of trespassing on the prohibited grounds. Would Dugan arrest him?

The captain held his gaze, challenging him to continue. Dugan rose, apparently gaining a better view of Bugsy, then sat again and returned his attention to Jamey. "Was this anywhere near the fires?"

"Prior to them, actually."

Together he and Shaylee explained the events, starting with the shooter and the bear trap—which Jamey withdrew from his backpack and handed to Dugan as proof—and went over the fire that drove them to the sinkhole, before concluding with the pickup wreck.

Dugan fingered the trap and leaned back in his chair. "I'll never understand why people break the law for the sheer pleasure of harming an innocent animal."

Jamey liked the gruff captain more with each passing minute.

Dugan glanced up to address Shaylee. "No doubt about it, Detective. If you hadn't prefaced this unbelievable tale with a warning, I'd have thought it was story hour at the library."

"Exactly," Shaylee said. "Sir, Baxter is responsible for the attacks on our lives."

Dugan's focus shifted between Jamey and Shaylee. "You saw your kidnapper?"

"No, sir, but I know Baxter ordered it."

"Detective." There was a warning in Dugan's tone. "Mr. Dyer, thank you for your brave efforts. I'm still curious how you happened to be in that specific location."

Shaylee jumped in. "He heard about the sinkholes, which matches his testimony."

Dugan stood and moved around the desk. "So you ignored the cordoned-off, prohibited park in search of sinkholes?"

Jamey exhaled. Time to own his decision and accept the consequences. "I went there specifically searching for Zia Heathcote's remains." He rushed on before he lost the gumption. "In my original testimony at Baxter Heathcote's trial, I stated that the *puparia* evidence located in the trunk of his SUV held traces of gypsum."

Dugan paused, leaning against the end of the desk. A hand on his chin. "That's right. I do remember your testimony."

Jamey's stomach tightened. "It—"

"—was quite impressive," Dugan concluded.

The air went out of Jamey's lungs like a popped balloon. "Unfortunately, it was refuted," he explained.

"Yes." Dugan shook his head. But the action didn't appear as condemnation, rather an understanding that Baxter's team had worked the system. "And when you two were in the bowels of the sinkhole, did you find anything to support your theory?"

"Yes and no. We located the gypsum mine, but we were more focused on getting out of there before the fire trapped us underground."

"I see." Dugan pushed off the desk. "I'll pretend I'm unaware of the illegal trespassing. Fire crews are still working the mountain, but I'll instruct them to look for the coffin. I wouldn't get your hopes up. Based on the last update, the devastation is severe."

"Sir, I respectfully request to continue investigating. With Jamey and Bugsy's help, we will find Zia."

Dugan shook his head. "There's not enough evidence

to support the connection. I can't authorize the investigation. And we cannot endanger a civilian's life."

"List him as a consultant."

"Negative. However, you're in danger, Adler. I'll make sure we have a unit patrol your neighborhood."

"No need, Captain—" Shaylee began.

"Nonnegotiable, Detective. Your safety is my biggest concern. Get your full report done ASAP."

Jamey's hadn't missed the way Captain Dugan's hardened expression had softened when he spotted the dogs. Though Dugan wasn't particularly inviting or approachable, his response to the animals told Jamey a lot about him.

"Bugsy rescued this little one in the mine before she led us to our escape route. We haven't named her yet." Shaylee glanced down at the pup. She spoke like they were a couple naming their child.

Why had his mind gone in that direction? "Speaking of, I contacted my veterinarian, and she has an opening. As soon as we're done here." He hoped the suggestion would move this little meeting along, as he had no desire to linger in the PD headquarters one second longer than necessary.

"The puppy is hurt?" Dugan asked, concern etching his face.

"Yes, she's favoring her right paw. Though I don't see an apparent break, I can't be totally sure," Jamey explained.

"Captain, Jamey's pickup was damaged, so we'll need a ride back to my place," Shaylee said.

Dugan shook his head.

Jamey felt his defenses rise again.

"No time for that. Let's wrap up so you all can take care of this little gal." He gently rubbed under the pup's chin. "Just borrow an unmarked vehicle. If you don't have a home for her, let me know."

Jamey gaped at the man's concern for the animal. "Thank you."

"Yes, sir," Shaylee replied, her tone defeated.

"Pleasure meeting you, Mr. Dyer," Captain Dugan said.

"Likewise." Jamey followed Shaylee to the reception-ist counter.

An older woman glanced up at their approach.

"This is Franny, receptionist/office manager/cat herder extraordinaire."

Franny pushed back from her desk and stood, barely reaching the top of the counter. She leaned across, smell-ing of coffee and pungent floral perfume. Her short hair was streaked with white, and looked stylish and stiff. She wore large yellow flower earrings. "I'm tellin' ya, Mrs. McNarly can ramble about nothing in particular, but get-ting a word in edgewise is near impossible. That woman needs a hobby." She held out a hand to Jamey. "Well, hey there, gorgeous. What's your name?"

Shaylee chuckled. "Franny is also a hopeless flirt."

Franny laughed. "Can't deny that."

"Jamey Dyer, ma'am. Pleased to meet you." He gently shook her hand. She had a strong grip that spoke of hard work.

"Oh, aren't you a love?" She winked at Jamey. "Shay-lee, honey, what happened to you?"

"Franny, it's a story worthy of a screenplay including being buried alive and surviving a fire."

The older lady's eyes widened. "What?"

Dugan approached from his office. "Didn't I tell you two to get outta here? Franny and I will notify the officers about your incident and get an APB out for the arsonist."

Franny spun. "Arsonist? Now I want details."

"We'll handle it," Dugan said, waving them off.

"Gotcha."

"I need to borrow the unmarked," Shaylee said.

Franny reached under the counter and produced a set of keys. "There you go, sweetness. Probably needs a fill up. A new guy had it last. He hasn't learned to clean and fill up the vehicles before he returns them." She turned to Jamey. "Takes a while to train the youngins."

"You'll soon have him eating out of the palm of your hand. Thanks, Franny. Have a good weekend." Shaylee touched Jamey's forearm.

"Very nice meeting you, ma'am," he said, smiling.

"You made my day, gorgeous," Franny said.

Jamey chuckled and followed Shaylee out the doors. "She's sweet."

"The best. Franny knows everything about everything. We'd be a mess without her."

They walked around the building's parking lot, and Shaylee approached a small blue sedan. She unlocked the doors with the key fob. Jamey loaded Bugsy in the back seat and took the pup from Shaylee, then slid inside.

"So, was it as bad as you expected?"

Jamey snapped his seat belt and settled the puppy in his lap. "No, but then most of the officers weren't in the building."

Shaylee adjusted her mirrors and seat belt, then started the car. "Sorry for Dugan's third degree. He seems gruff, but he's a real softy inside."

"Actually, I didn't mind him at all. He clearly has a heart for animals, and that boosts his credibility with me," Jayme replied.

"Where to?"

"Piedmont."

Shaylee headed to the highway. The pup whined, and Jamey glanced down. "Her nose is too dry."

"That's not a good thing, is it?"

"No. I'm praying Dr. Keough will give us an easy resolution for her."

Something had to go right today.

"Have you picked a name for her?" Shaylee asked.

"Hmm." Jamey tilted his head. "What do you think of Echo?"

"I like it."

"Echo, what's your vote?" He stroked her downy fur, and she yawned. Jamey grinned. "I guess that's acceptable to her. Bugsy?"

She gave a sharp bark and Jamey laughed. "A definite yes."

"If I didn't know better, I'd believe you actually understand them." Shaylee smiled, capturing his attention. She was so beautiful.

He looked away. *Don't get attached.* Their time together was nearly finished.

"I've never named a dog with anyone."

"Me, either." *That's the best reply you can muster?*

"It's kind of a bonding experience, don't you think?"

Ugh. No. No, it's not. An awkward pause hung between them. Jamey reached over and flipped on the radio, desperate to fill the quiet before he said something stupid or found ways to continue working with her. A love song emanated from the speakers. The singer wailed about how much he wanted to proclaim his feelings for the gorgeous woman who was oblivious to his existence. He quickly scrolled the stations looking for a different genre.

"Not into country?" Shaylee asked.

"Uh, just prefer a little more upbeat tune." And deflect the irrational thoughts bombarding him.

Once they took care of Echo's medical needs, Shaylee would drop him off and they'd go their separate ways.

That was best for everyone.

Wasn't it?

EIGHT

Disappointment overrode Shaylee's relief as she pulled into town. After all they'd endured, the prospect of separation should've ushered in a reprieve, yet being in Jamey's company just felt right, as though they'd known each other for years, rather than hours. And after she dropped him off, she would have no real reason to see him or talk to him again. Their time together had ended, and the realization weighed on her.

"Thanks again for driving us all over South Dakota."

Did she detect a hint of sadness in Jamey's smile? Probably just wishful thinking on her part.

"It was the least I could do."

A dark van approached faster than necessary behind them, catching Shaylee's eye and causing the hair on her neck to stiffen. She made a turn onto a side street, and the vehicle did the same.

"I don't mean to be a backseat driver, but I live on the other side of town," Jamey said.

Shaylee's gaze bounced between the road ahead and the rearview mirror. She took a last-minute turn again, this time heading north. "Don't look now but I think we might have company. I'm taking the back way to the PD. Let's see if he follows."

Jamey's gaze shifted to the side mirror. "I can't see

the driver from here with the window tint and reflecting sunlight."

"And how convenient there's no front license plate, either. Are the dogs okay?"

"Yes, they're both asleep on the back seat," Jamey confirmed.

She neared the alley behind the parking lot and caught a glimpse of the driver's baseball cap and sunglasses disguising his appearance as he zoomed past, apparently unconcerned about her suspicions. "Well, that was weird."

"He's gone."

"I would say I overreacted, but my gut doesn't agree." Shaylee called the information in to dispatch as a precaution, then made a U-turn and merged on the main road. "Let's take a little detour and see if our friend returns. I don't want to lead him to your house."

"Sounds good to me."

With no sign of the van, Shaylee proceeded through town toward Jamey's house, going the long way. "I don't like this part of town," she said as they entered the lower district of older homes and businesses. Graffiti covered walls and trash littered the streets. She knew too much about crimes committed in the area.

She approached a cement viaduct tunnel under the two-lane road. "I forgot we'd have to go under that," she said, suddenly wary of her choice of route.

"I haven't seen the van since we stopped by the PD. Besides, how would he know we'd come this way?" Jamey replied.

Shaylee didn't respond, accelerating to get to the other side as fast as the speed limit allowed.

When they emerged safely on the opposite side, she exhaled, not realizing she'd held her breath.

But her relief dissipated at the sight of the familiar van

parked beneath the shadows of a mature tree ahead. "He's back."

A man stepped from behind the vehicle, holding a sniper rifle.

"Get down!"

Several consecutive shots sounded as they passed, pelting the vehicle and shattering the back window. Shaylee swerved and whipped through an abandoned building's parking lot and down an alley onto the street.

The revving of an engine preceded the van's pursuit.

"Call it in!" She tossed Jamey her phone.

He shrank low in the seat and reported the incident. His voice merged with more gunshots and the car jerked.

"He's hit a tire!" Shaylee gripped the wheel, fighting to stay on the road. The front end of the car slammed into a large pothole before bouncing onto the gravel again.

"The dispatcher said an officer is near."

Shaylee circled outside of town, not wanting to endanger innocent passersby.

A siren's approaching scream brought slight relief and a deterrent. The van veered, turning and disappearing between two buildings.

Shaylee continued on a few more minutes until she was certain the van wasn't following anymore, then pulled over on the side of the road. "Are you all right?"

Jamey nodded and sat up in the seat. "I want to check on the girls."

They got out, released the dogs and inspected them for injuries. Both were wide-eyed, but neither had sustained cuts from the glass.

Shaylee retrieved a blanket from the trunk and placed it on the seat to protect the animals from the shattered glass. While Jamey got them situated, she called in to the PD, notifying the dispatcher of their status.

"They didn't catch the guy, but there's a BOLO for the van," she told Jamey.

"Let's get the dogs back to my house. We're too exposed out here."

"Agreed."

The drive was quiet and once Shaylee pulled up in front of Jamey's house, she was more determined than ever to separate. She was a moving target and had put them all in danger.

She turned off the ignition and faced him. "I've had enough adventure for one day."

"Same here."

"I am so glad Echo will be okay."

"Dr. Keough is the best." Jamey glanced down at the pup with a bandaged paw. "Just a minor sprain and dehydration. We'll get her back to a hundred percent in no time, right, Bugsy?"

On cue, the bluetick coonhound poked her head between the seats, tail thumping in conceding rhythm.

Shaylee grinned, admiring Jamey's communication style with animals. "I'm impressed you identified Echo as a border collie before Dr. Keough did."

"Border collie mix," Jamey corrected. "She's got all the typical features. They're an intelligent breed. I have big plans for her."

Bugsy whined.

Shaylee slid her fingers through the dog's soft mane. "I think you hurt her feelings."

"There's no comparison to you, Bugs," he said, scratching the dog's floppy ears.

"I've only had cats for pets. Bugsy is the first animal I've witnessed who actually likes her vet. It took my dad, mom, Zia, me and my grandmother to get our cat into a carrier for her appointments. She had a sixth sense or something."

Jamey laughed. "Animals are incredibly intuitive. However, I'm guessing she saw the carrier and anticipated the trip. Unless you took her places often?"

Shaylee considered his argument. "When you put it that way, the logic seems obvious. Wish I'd known you twenty years ago. It would have saved me a lot of scratches."

Jamey snorted. "Trust me, you wouldn't have even given me a second glance twenty years ago."

"What makes you think that?"

"I wasn't always the stellar specimen you see before you." He made an exaggerated effort to puff out his chest.

She chuckled. "Do tell."

"I weighed eighty pounds soaking wet, I wore enormous glasses resembling the bottom of a soda bottle, and my hand-me-down pants were always a tad too short for my ever-growing legs. Although that was no fault of my shorter older brothers."

"Such is the plight of the younger sibling. Zia was shorter than me, too. My parents claimed buying me new clothes was a waste of money since I'd outgrow them too fast." Unexpected sadness at the memory of Momma and Zia returning home with bags from their many shopping trips stabbed her heart.

"Yeah, but you probably made them look good." Shaylee met Jamey's eyes and his cheeks flushed. "I, on the other hand, was a class A nerd."

A quick perusal, and she blurted, "Whatever. I seriously doubt that."

"Trust me, I had twelve years of classmates verify the title." The vulnerability in his voice touched her. "It's hard to be cool when your closest friends have six or more legs." He waggled his eyebrows, and she chuckled.

"Honestly, you're probably right. I wouldn't have talked to you, but not because of your reasons. My preoccupation with making myself invisible had become top priority."

"You? Why?"

She sighed. "Zia cast a long shadow."

"I have to admit, if I hadn't known Zia was your sister, I might not have believed it."

Jamey's words ignited a volcano of bitterness in Shaylee with the all too familiar reminder that she would always be plain, unattractive Shaylee next to jaw-droppingly stunning Zia. The emotions erupted, and she shoved open her door. "Yes, I've heard that most of my life."

She exited the car and walked to the trunk to retrieve Echo's supplies.

Jamey was out and at her side in record time. "Here, take Echo, and I'll get those." He passed the puppy to her and reached into the trunk. "I have two brothers, and we all looked alike except for the height difference. It was like getting us in triplicate." He spoke in rapid speed, clearly flustered. "But we've changed as we aged. Let me get Bugsy—" He continued rambling as he opened the back passenger door, releasing the dog.

Shaylee didn't hear him over her chastising conscience. Jamey wasn't responsible for her issues. She'd unfairly unleashed her hang-ups on him with her reaction.

"—only benefit was immersing myself in the study of insects. I may or may not have retaliated by introducing grasshoppers to the guys who bullied me. Even football players will scream when a bucketful of grasshoppers burst out of their locker unexpectedly."

Shaylee interrupted Jamey before the poor guy rambled himself hoarse with stories. "Don't mind my sibling rivalry issues. It occasionally pokes its ugly head into conversations unannounced."

He blinked. "I'm really sorry, Shaylee. I didn't mean to offend you." The kindness in his blue irises nearly undid her.

"It's not you. Normally, I'm not so touchy, I'm just tired, which is a lousy excuse to not control my mouth."

He leaned against the car. "We don't have to talk about Zia anymore."

"No, I want to." Surprised by her own confession, she snuggled Echo under her chin, relishing the softness of her fur. Did she want to tell him? Something about Jamey made talking to him easy. Would sharing her pain release her from the plaguing insecurity she'd carried regarding Zia? "My parents took special effort in exhibiting Zia's beauty to everyone within a two-hundred-mile radius. She was always drop-dead gorgeous. But for the record, we are biological siblings. Zia took after my mother, petite and delicate. I got more of my father's masculine characteristics." Shaylee looked down at her boots and pants, the clothing only emphasizing her point. And now she'd unloaded way more information than she'd intended. *Stop talking before he sees just how damaged you really are.*

Jamey laughed. "You're kidding, right?"

She focused too intently on a spot near her foot, avoiding his eyes.

His finger gently lifted her chin, and she met his gaze. "There's nothing masculine about you, Shaylee. You're beautiful."

Befuddled by his compliment, she stood mute. No man had said such kind things to her. Not even Daddy.

Jamey's ears had blended into a bright crimson hue, and for a second, she thought he might kiss her or take off running in the opposite direction. She wasn't sure which she'd prefer until he leaned toward her.

Shaylee sucked in a breath.

Sandalwood lingered in the air. He paused, locking gazes with her. His lips parted slightly.

Her pulse raced; her mouth went desert-dry.

Then he reached toward her.

Shaylee braced for his touch.

Her knees weakened.

Instead of kissing her, Jamey reached into the trunk and lifted out the supplies, then spun around and headed for the front porch.

Confusion collided with her expectations. She watched his retreating form and exhaled a soft snort. Totally misjudged that one. Shaylee closed the lid. Embarrassment at her assumption fueled her steps. She trailed him to where Bugsy sat waiting patiently.

Jamey inserted a key and pushed open the door, allowing Shaylee to enter first. "Did Zia model or enter beauty pageants?"

"Both. If there was any opportunity to show off Zia, my parents signed her up."

"Sounds like they were the culprits, rather than Zia seeking attention?"

They entered his house, and he set the box on the floor.

Shaylee closed the door. "I think there were times she enjoyed it. Why wouldn't she? I can't blame her. Although occasionally, she complained about them dragging her from one event to another. Ironically, Baxter paraded her around the same way."

"Were you close in age?"

"She was three years older."

Jamey withdrew Echo's new dog bed from the box and walked to the far side of the living and dining room combination. He set it beside the larger dog bed positioned against the wall, surrounded by an assortment of toys and a bone. "Did you get toted around with them?"

Shaylee settled Echo on the soft pad, missing her instantly. "No. My grandmother lived with us, so I stayed home with her. We had a lot of quality time together. Some of my happiest memories are of our talks, baking and gardening."

Bugsy joined them, sniffed Echo, then flopped onto her own bed.

"I think she's glad to be home," Shaylee said.

"Definitely."

She surveyed the spotless bungalow. "Your house is delightful."

"It's small but works for us. Three bedrooms, one bathroom. Not much to see."

Simple furnishings comprised the space, including a worn overstuffed recliner and matching couch positioned opposite a mounted television. A coffee table placed in the middle of the room held a remote control and a neat stack of library books.

Jamey hoisted the box and disappeared behind a wall separating what Shaylee guessed was the kitchen. She followed him past a wooden dining table with a rectangular planter in the center holding live succulents.

"Did you always dislike Baxter?"

Shaylee entered the kitchen. "At first, he was charming and articulate. Treated Zia like a princess. Honestly, I was jealous. But then something changed. Zia withdrew from family events, making excuses for her absences. It wasn't like her. Baxter controlled her every move. I spoke up, and that made us instant enemies. He doesn't like women voicing their opinions."

"I'd have to agree. Baxter surrounds himself with yes-men. But I'd think he'd strive to be in good graces with you all. If nothing else, to maintain appearances."

"Oh, he did until our folks passed. Then with just me, he didn't bother anymore." She leaned against the counter, equally impressed with the pristine kitchen. "Wow, my grandmother would say your floor is so clean you can eat off it." Not a crumb littered the countertop, and there were no smudges on the tiled floor, not even a magnet on the fridge.

Jamey grinned. "I'm kind of compulsive when it comes to neatness. I blame my mother. Her philosophy was never touch something twice. If you pick up a dirty dish, wash it and put it away all at once. I can't say I'm that fanatical, but I appreciate things in their rightful place." He moved to the counter and ripped into the small bag of puppy food, opened a can of wet dog food and mixed them.

"You can't give Echo Bugsy's food?"

At the mention of their names, nails clicked on the tile, announcing the arrival of both dogs.

"Puppies need extra fat and nutrients. Plus, with her baby teeth, she might find Bugsy's food too large and hard to chew." Jamey opened the antibiotic pill bottle the veterinarian had provided. He dropped a large tablet into the bowl, using the food to conceal it.

"Can I help?"

"Sure, if you want to. They both need fresh water." Jamey opened the pantry door and scooped dry food into Bugsy's bowl.

Shaylee filled the dishes Jamey provided and set them on the floor. It was so easy being with him; they worked together seamlessly.

Stop that. They weren't a couple. Not an option. He didn't like cops, and she was working a case. End of story.

Bugsy immediately went to her bowl. Echo watched curiously before meandering to her food. She eyeballed and sniffed the offerings warily, then lapped the water. Bugsy had already finished her food by the time Echo conceded to take the plunge.

Shaylee laughed. "I guess she approves."

Jamey smiled. "That's a good sign."

"Will you need a ride to pick up your truck tomorrow?"

"No. My mechanic, Cody, said he'd have someone drop it off for me when he's done."

She worked to hide her disappointment. "I'm glad the brakes were the extent of the damage."

"Yeah, me, too. By the way, thanks for the detour to the phone store. Good thing I had it insured." He withdrew his new phone.

Shaylee nodded. "Not a problem. Program in my number." Had she just said that aloud?

"Why?"

She blinked, unsure how to respond. Why did she want him to have her phone number? "I'd love an update on Echo," she blurted.

"Oh, right. Um, sure." Jamey entered the number Shaylee provided. "I'll send a text message so you have mine, too."

"My phone is probably blowing up at home."

He smiled while cleaning up. She helped put away the dog food and leaned against the counter.

"So, what will you do next?"

"Shower." She swiped a hand through her hair, fully aware she looked terrible.

"Good idea. I need to do the same."

Shaylee scanned him, taking a little too long. Even after the day they'd had, he didn't appear disheveled at all.

"You look deep in thought." Jamey turned, reached into the refrigerator and withdrew a bottle of water, passing it to her, and grabbed one for himself. "I really need to make a trip to the store."

Shaylee took the water. "Thanks."

Why was she prolonging her departure? She needed to walk away, leave Jamey alone and pray Baxter wouldn't bother him. A part—a huge, annoying, very loud part—of her wanted to continue working with him. They shared a common goal of finding Zia.

Except as a walking target, she needed to keep her distance. The less she involved Jamey, the better. But the need to share the burden she carried weighed on her. Was it fair to involve Jamey? She sipped the water, delaying and contemplating.

"Are you okay? You got all quiet. Did I say something wrong? Again?" Jamey sipped his water. "It's a gift." He quirked a brow and made a silly face.

Now she'd done it. If she brushed off the conversation, he'd assume she was lying or avoiding him. There was no going back now. She had to tell him about the journal. And then what? *Oh, by the way, there's this clue, but never mind, I'll handle it, so don't worry about it?*

It had been pure selfishness to drag him into her mess. Sadness hovered over her. But not involving Jamey was the right thing to do. Baxter wanted her dead. And she couldn't risk Jamey's life any more than she already had.

This was her battle, and she would fight it.

"Shaylee? Please talk to me."

The words warred with her reasoning, the tender concern in his blue eyes chipping away at her armor. He touched her arm. "Please?"

She shook her head, reminding herself to shut up. But the words flew out before she could contain them. "There's something I need to tell you."

Jamey waited for Shaylee to continue, but she remained silent. "Am I supposed to guess?" he teased, hoping to snap her out of the muted state.

"Sorry, I just… Disregard."

"Aw, c'mon, you can't do that to me. Let's move to the living room where it's more comfortable." He didn't wait for her to respond, and walked to his recliner.

She strolled to the sofa and lowered onto the cushion, apprehension in her expression.

His mind traversed the universe of possibilities. What did she mean? What hadn't she told him? Would she arrest him for trespassing at Black Hills National Forest? No. She'd have done it a long time ago.

"At least give me a clue. If you don't talk, I'll be forced to regale you with more of my childhood antics."

She gave a shaky smile and exhaled, straightening her posture. "In all the excitement and busyness of trying to survive today, then handling Echo's care and getting you a new phone, I didn't—" She looked down, fidgeting with the bottle. "No, that's not true. I'm dancing around the topic and making excuses."

"Well, you're confusing me, that's for sure."

"Jamey, I didn't want to burden you with any more of the baggage in Zia's case. I'm the killer's target, not you."

"I'd beg to differ—"

She shook her head. "You're collateral damage from his attempts on my life."

"That might be how it started, but he made it personal from the first gunshot fired at me and Bugsy." Didn't she understand he cared? What baggage from Zia's case was she talking about?

"I know the attacks are focused on me. Once we go our separate ways, I think, I hope, I pray you and the dogs will be safe again."

Jamey perched on the edge of the recliner. "And what if we're not? What if he's got his eye on us, too? Shaylee, I want to find Zia. And no offense, but I'm doing that with or without you. If there are clues to help me, I'd like to know."

"I want that, too, but this won't help you find Zia."

"How can you be certain unless you tell me?"

"You don't have what he wants. I do."

"And I'm assuming 'he' refers to Baxter?"

"Yes."

Frustrated but determined to get her talking, he reasoned, "You can't be one hundred percent certain Baxter is the one after you. I don't like the guy, either, but Zia's trial ended a long time ago. Why sprout up now and specifically target you?"

Shaylee tilted her head. "It's Baxter or at least an extension of his efforts. I'm working through the lead. If I could connect the evidence with Baxter, I'd haul him away today."

"What evidence? What does he want from you?"

She took another sip, and Jamey restrained himself from ripping the bottle out of her hand and begging her to speak. Instead, he practiced patience. When he was at the point of bursting with curiosity, she spoke.

"Let's start with the timing. I confronted Baxter last night, before my abduction, over a portion of an accounting journal."

The dogs moseyed in and moved to their beds.

Shaylee shifted to the edge of the couch. "I found a torn page inside Zia's childhood Bible. I'm not an accountant, so, to be honest, I'm not sure what it means, but it was important enough for Zia to hide it there."

Jamey took a sip and studied the bottle. "When you confronted Baxter, did he flip out?"

Shaylee harrumphed. "Baxter would never lower himself by appearing anything other than perfectly composed. His bodyguard shoved me out the door before I got a confession out of him. But that was prior to me waking up in the coffin. The timing isn't coincidental."

Interesting. "I agree. So why didn't you share this with me earlier? I mean not that it would've helped us on the mountain, but it's a clue for sure."

A shadow passed over her face, and she averted her eyes. "I didn't want to involve you more than you already are. And this explains why I need to continue on this quest alone."

He gripped the water bottle, causing the plastic to crackle in his hand. She couldn't continue this mission without his help. Except all he brought to the table was science. He was no mighty warrior, and he couldn't protect her with a microscope and chromatographs. "Two minds are better than one."

"I can't do that. Once you're removed from the equation, you won't be in danger anymore. Baxter wants me dead. Not you."

Separated from Shaylee was the worst scenario. He appealed to her sense of reasoning. "I'd like to get a look at this journal. I may see something you missed?"

Conflict warred in her hazel eyes. Great. He'd added to her burdens. Placed her in an impossible situation. He wasn't law enforcement, and he wasn't allowed to contribute to the investigation. She couldn't qualify him as an expert or even a consultant on the case, since he had no accounting background.

She bit her lip, and before she could reject his ridiculously bold and unallowable request, he blurted, "Actually, you're right. I really am not the one to help. Never mind."

"I'm sorry, forget about it. Please. I shouldn't have said anything about the journal." She rose. "I'd better go."

Taken aback, Jamey stood, too. Hadn't he released her from the obligation? Why did she want to leave? "Why?"

It wasn't about the journal or a conflict of interest for him. Shaylee had reapplied her law enforcement shield, shutting him out.

She didn't trust him. And why should she? He was a joke to her comrades, and he hadn't done a great job of protecting her. She'd nearly died three times in his company. Shaylee didn't want him involved because she didn't trust his judgment. She needed an equal, and that wasn't him.

Pressuring her was wrong. He had no right to demand anything of her.

But he'd continue searching for Zia without Shaylee. Once he found her, Jamey would have the evidence to take down Baxter. That was the way he'd protect her. Not with brawn, but with intelligence.

Convinced of his plan, he said, "No problem. I understand. You should get home and rest." He moved to the door and opened it.

"Right. Okay."

Was that relief he saw in her expression? Of course it was. He'd just let her off the hook, and before he changed his mind and pleaded with her to stay, he had to get Shaylee Adler out of his house. He wouldn't want to do anything that added to her already stressful position.

But he didn't want to eliminate their connection.

Jamey stuffed his hands into his jeans pockets to keep from pulling her into his arms. "However, if you hear from the fire investigators and the coffin is accessible, I'd still like to figure out what drew Bugsy there. I won't interfere with whatever is left of the crime scene."

Not entirely true, but he didn't need her permission or assistance to survey the scene. He had a right to know what had attracted or distracted Bugsy and the cockroach he'd seen in the coffin was a clue.

"Yes, of course. I'll call first thing in the morning." Shaylee paused in the doorway. "Take care. I'll talk to you later."

She hesitated by the sedan and glanced at him. Jamey offered a short wave. Everything within him wanted to retract his words. Beg her to let him help.

He waited until she'd slid behind the wheel of her car before he closed the door. Jamey moved to the living room and watched through the blinds until the vehicle disappeared from sight.

Bugsy moved to his side and nudged his hand. "I miss her already, too." She tilted her head as if to say, *Go after Shaylee*. Or maybe that was Jamey's wishful thinking. "I can't," he mumbled. With a sigh, Bugsy returned to her dog bed. Echo snored softly, already submerged in her new life.

This was his world. Dogs. They didn't abandon or reject him. They didn't question his ability or his competence.

And yet, he still felt so alone.

Jamey wandered into the kitchen and grabbed his new cell phone from the kitchen counter.

He glanced at the screen and swiped to read the message he'd sent to Shaylee. Cringing, he stared at the words. Hi, it's Jamey Dyer.

What a dork. Someone needed to invent a way to edit an already sent message. Apparently, he was just as awkward in texting as he was in person. Good to know.

His emotions were all over the place. Anger swirled because Shaylee didn't trust him with the clues from Zia's investigation. She didn't trust him enough to include him and allow him to look at the journal.

Frustrated he hadn't handled the discussion better, Jamey considered all the ways he should have negotiated, pleaded, anything rather than escorting her to the door.

Did the accounting journal matter that much to him? It wasn't as though he knew anything about accounting. But it wasn't about the journal.

He wanted to protect Shaylee.

His emotions played a cruel game of tug-of-war. Was she better off without him? He didn't deserve to work with Shaylee, anyway. She'd been too kind to speak the words, but he was fully aware of his inadequacies. And her hesitation spoke of her distrust. Even after everything they'd been through.

Disappointment in himself hurt more. Keep law enforcement at a distance. Arm's length. They weren't in the same league.

Still, he contemplated, had he jumped to conclusions? Was he misreading the whole situation?

No, she'd refrained from speaking. Better that he was the one to acknowledge the situation. He'd prevented her from telling him he wasn't privy to the information.

Yet, they'd shared a pleasant afternoon and being with Shaylee had been comfortable. He'd enjoyed the day, well, after they'd stopped fighting for their lives and dodging danger.

She'd seemed interested in him. A twinge of hope that perhaps Shaylee had intentionally prolonged their departure had him grinning, but he shoved it down. They'd talked like friends. Until he stuck his boot in his mouth with the comment about her not looking like Zia.

Jamey slapped his forehead. Good going. No, she couldn't be interested in someone like him.

Shaylee was an attractive, capable woman. Yet he saw a vulnerability, an insecurity beneath the tough exterior. Hard to imagine her being jealous of her sister. He didn't understand women, but he understood sibling rivalry. He and his brothers always one-upped each other. Until they'd stopped one-upping each other altogether.

He strolled through the house to the spare bedroom and lifted the picture of him and his brothers from the bookshelf. They hadn't spoken in years. How would he even start a conversation after all this time? Neither of them had tried contacting him. But what if something happened, and they didn't get another chance?

He remembered the way they'd laughed and the hard times when they'd protected each other from their father's mighty wrath. They'd silently agreed being together was too painful a reminder.

Maybe he would try to contact them.

After he found Zia.

He replaced the picture and sulked down the hallway to check on the dogs. Both lay sprawled, feet twitching in a dreaming state. Probably running. He grinned when

Bugsy's snore bounced off the walls. She had serious lungs and had earned rest.

Sweet and content. He shuddered to think what would've happened if they hadn't found Echo. Had she run away or had her owners abandoned her? His experience left him jaded, assuming the worst.

Echo gave a muffled bark in her sleep.

"Yeah, you tell 'em, sister," he whispered. Should he text a picture of them to Shaylee?

Now he was coming up with excuses to communicate with her. He wanted the connection but didn't want to be pushy.

No, the truth was he didn't want to be rejected.

And it didn't matter.

Tomorrow, as soon as he got his truck back, he'd return to Black Hills National Forest and continue searching for Zia's body.

Alone.

And by doing what he could, he'd protect Shaylee from Baxter or whoever was after her.

Because he had to protect Shaylee.

Somehow.

NINE

Shaylee studied the torn accounting journal page and popped a handful of popcorn into her mouth. Her favorite after dinner snack and healthier than the fast-food burger she'd eaten two hours earlier. The clue was right in front of her face, she just needed to find it. Again, she contemplated contacting Jamey. Maybe he would see something she missed? No, dragging him into her mess was selfish.

The chime of her cell phone sent hope dancing. Jamey? Dugan's name appeared on the screen. Chewing and swallowing as fast as possible, Shaylee set down the paper and answered, "Sir."

"Fire investigators have cleared the scene and confirmed that the melted remnants of what I assume was the coffin were destroyed."

Shaylee dropped onto the couch. "Fantastic," she mumbled sarcastically. An idea sprouted. "Jamey requested to return to the site to search for what attracted Bugsy there in the first place. She might locate something they overlooked."

"Doubtful anything is left, but so long as you follow procedure, I have no issues."

"Thanks."

"How's the pup doing?"

She grinned. Animals and children brought out Dugan's softer side.

"Dr. Keough diagnosed Echo—that's what Jamey named her—with a sprained leg, but says she'll heal quickly."

"That's good news. I authorized a unit to patrol your neighborhood."

A knock on the back door jolted her. "Thank you, but really I'm fine. I appreciate the update, Captain. Someone's here, so I gotta go."

"Stay on the phone with me while you look to see who it is. Don't open that door yet."

Slightly annoyed but grateful Dugan cared about her safety, she hurried to the kitchen and peered through the corner of the closed blinds. Noreen Liddle stood on the patio deck, shifting nervously from one foot to another.

Noreen and her grandmother were longtime friends of the Adler family. However, serving as Baxter's intern pitted Noreen between loyalty to her employer and her friendship with Shaylee, making their communication secretive.

"It's just Noreen, and since Baxter's behind my abduction, I'm sure he's watching to ensure his plan worked."

"Adler—"

"I know, I know."

"Keep me updated," Dugan said before disconnecting.

Shaylee placed her cell phone on the counter and opened the door. "Hey, what're you doing here?"

"Can I come in?" Noreen glanced over her shoulder.

"Sure." Shaylee stepped aside, allowing the young intern to scurry past. Before closing the door, she peered into the darkened yard. "Why the back door?"

"I didn't want anyone to see me and have word get back to Baxter."

"Where did you park?"

"Around the corner. I would've come sooner, but I

couldn't get away. I heard about the abduction. Were you seriously buried alive?" Noreen pulled Shaylee into a bear hug.

Leaning back, Shaylee asked, "How did you hear about it?"

"Franny," Noreen said as if that explained everything. In a way, it did. Franny was aware of their friendship and wouldn't think twice about sharing the information. She wasn't malicious, but she was the town crier.

"Yeah, but I'm fine now."

Noreen released her hold and moved to the wingback chair in the living room. "You're amazingly strong to survive that! Did you see who did it? Have they arrested anyone?"

"I have my suspicions… Speaking of, how's your boss?"

"Baxter wouldn't do anything so insidious."

"Don't underestimate him." Shaylee paused by the kitchen counter. "Want a cup of chamomile tea?"

Noreen wrinkled her nose. "No, thanks. But the popcorn smells delicious."

"Help yourself. Chamomile tea? It's great for relaxing before bed."

"Even if you drink it every night?" Noreen gave a sideways grin.

Shaylee shrugged. "What can I say? I'm a creature of habit. At this point, I don't think I could sleep without it. Water? Soda?"

"No, I'm good."

Shaylee slid to her favorite spot on the sofa and sat, feet tucked under her.

"How did you get away?" Noreen grabbed a handful of popcorn.

"It's a very long story. A wonderful cadaver dog and her handler, Jamey, rescued me."

"Like in dead people?" Noreen blinked several times behind her oversize glasses.

"Yep. We also found an injured puppy. She's the most adorable little thing."

"Are you smiling because of the dog or her handler?" Noreen gave her a conspiratorial grin.

Shaylee waved her off. "The puppy. I cannot stop thinking about her." Or Jamey.

"Where is she?" Noreen looked around the room.

"Jamey kept her. His dog, Bugsy, will help train Echo. That's the puppy. But when she's ready, I'm hoping Jamey will allow me to adopt her."

"If I weren't deathly allergic, I'd beg to see her."

Shaylee gave a sympathetic tilt of her head. "I forgot about that."

"No biggie. Always wanted pets, but there's not enough allergy medicine in the world to make it possible."

"Didn't you have a turtle as a kid?"

"Yeah. He wasn't fun to cuddle, though." Noreen grabbed another handful of popcorn and munched. "So how did Jamey and Bugsy find you? Didn't the state close the area because of those sinkholes?"

Shaylee nodded and yawned. "Forgive me, but I've had a day like you wouldn't believe. I promise to give you the ugly details when I'm more awake."

Noreen leaned forward. "Of course. You should rest. I'm worried about you. Why didn't you call me?"

"You're sweet to come by." Shaylee deliberately ignored the question.

"I figured if the lights were off, you were asleep, and I wouldn't bother you."

"It's eight thirty—I don't crash that early." Shaylee yawned again. "Although tonight might be an exception." She hugged a throw pillow and forced a casual tone into her voice. "So, how did Baxter react after his bodyguard threw me out last night?"

"He was furious." Noreen fidgeted with her hands, then bit on a fingernail.

"Stop that," Shaylee admonished.

"Sorry, nasty habit." Noreen pushed her navy-framed glasses—too large and masculine for her round, childlike face—farther up on her hooked nose. Then she tugged down her white cardigan and smoothed the plain navy skirt, looking more like an adolescent than a twenty-one-year-old intern.

"Are you okay? Did Baxter hurt you?"

Noreen shook her head vehemently. "No, he'd never do that."

"He's a dangerous man. Don't underestimate him. You really should get away from Baxter. There are other jobs in South Dakota."

"He was cleared of Zia's murder," Noreen stated softly, looking down. A section of her mousy brown hair swept over one shoulder.

"A technicality and mistake on the prosecutors' part." Though Shaylee detested Baxter, Noreen's loyalty was commendable. She'd never spoken ill of anyone. It would do no good to press the issue. Besides, Noreen was the furthest thing from a threat to the senator-elect.

Noreen resumed chewing on her fingernail. "Did you really find evidence against him?"

Shaylee hesitated. Noreen's ability to access Baxter's financial records was an immense benefit. Her gaze flitted to the document on the table, and she passed it to Noreen. "I found this."

"What is it?" She studied the small section of paper, and her eyes narrowed.

"The paper dropped out of Zia's childhood Bible, as though it had been waiting for me all this time. I think

Zia discovered Baxter's illegal financial methods. He's a thieving murderer. And somehow, I'm going to prove it." Shaylee held out her hand and took back the paper.

"I miss her, too." Noreen's tone was gentle.

Tears welled in Shaylee's eyes at her kind understanding, and she blinked them away. "I have to find Zia and bring her home."

"You deserve peace," Noreen whispered. "What can I do to help?"

The offer had Shaylee's full attention. "Really?"

"You and Zia were like my big sisters. Since Grandma's passing, you're the only family I have left. Without Zia speaking up for me, I never would've landed the job as Baxter's intern. I owe you both. It's the most rewarding part of my life."

Shaylee's smile quivered. "Do you have access to Baxter's financials? Anything that might prove illegal funding?"

"I'll do my best. But—" She worried the fingernail again. "He'll fire me if he finds out."

"I don't want that. Just poke around without compromising your position. It'll be between us."

"On one condition. If I find nothing, promise me you'll stop accusing Baxter of Zia's murder. I know you think he's a terrible man, but I see a different side of him."

Shaylee gaped at the young intern. "I wish I had your optimism, but everything within me is certain he's guilty. I just need the evidence to prove it." Noreen frowned, and Shaylee rushed on, "But if you'll help me, I promise to take your view into consideration. I wouldn't want to prosecute an innocent man."

That seemed to lighten the mood slightly. Noreen pushed off the chair and stood. "I understand. I'd better go."

Encouraged, Shaylee followed her to the back door. "I'll walk you to your car."

"I'll be fine."

"Dugan ordered a unit to patrol this area. Did you see him?" Shaylee asked.

Noreen tilted her head. "No, but maybe I missed him while he was cruising the neighborhood."

A definite possibility, but something tugged at Shaylee. "Thanks for coming by." She hugged her friend and watched as Noreen disappeared into the shadows before closing and locking the door. She leaned against it. "Lord, You promised justice. I've dedicated my life to finding Zia, and I can't do it without You. Thank You for Noreen's willingness to help me. Bring the truth to light."

Noreen's access to Baxter would give Shaylee the evidence she needed to take down the criminal. Once and for all.

Or she'd made a horrible mistake. Would Noreen cave under pressure if caught going through his records? For a brief moment, the worry she'd confessed to the wrong person lingered in her mind.

No. Their long friendship spoke for itself.

Stifling another yawn, Shaylee grabbed her cell phone, turned off the lights and walked to her bedroom. She set the phone on her nightstand and completed her bathroom routine before sliding between the cool cotton sheets. Her body relaxed, releasing the stress and adventure of the day, and she drifted off to sleep.

A creak and thud dragged her awake like the daggered claws from the coyotes the night before.

She bolted upright in her bed and shoved off the covers. Just a nightmare.

She was safe. In her bedroom.

The ambient glow from the streetlight outside filtered

in through her partially open window and a breeze fluttered the curtain.

She glanced at the door.

The hairs stood up on her neck and arms, and all senses were on high alert.

She held her breath as the distant ruffling reached her from beyond the hallway.

It was no dream.

An intruder was in her house!

Shaylee struggled to focus over her pulse's violent drumming. Without a visual, she couldn't determine the intruder's precise location inside her home.

A quick glance at the clock on her nightstand revealed it was 3:10 a.m.

Her biggest advantage was the intruder was unaware she'd awoken.

The curtains swayed gently. There was always the option of climbing out the window and running for help.

Shaylee clutched the sheets. No way. If this was the same guy who'd abducted and buried her, she'd delight in taking him down.

Resolve forced away the fear. With her gaze transfixed on the door, she caught sight of a barely perceptible glow. It swept past the hallway, casting a ghostly shadow on the opposite wall.

Was there more than one person?

Call for backup.

Eyes fixed on the doorway, she slid one hand to the nightstand, searching for her cell phone. Her fingers grazed the cool glass display, and she opened her palm to grasp the device. Her loaded department-issued Colt M 1911 sat ready, beckoning her.

And out of reach, across the room on her dresser.

Light in the hallway shifted, glowing brighter.

He was coming!

Shaylee jerked, miscalculating the phone's location.

It teetered before slipping out of her hold.

The device dropped off the nightstand, bouncing twice on the hardwood floor.

She froze. The double thuds shattered the silence of the night.

He'd no doubt heard her.

Shaylee scrambled off the bed.

She crept to the dresser and stretched to grasp the Colt. The familiar coolness of the weapon gave her comfort as she inched toward the door, hiding in the shadows. Gun at the ready, she prepared to enter the hallway, aware she'd be exposed.

One last glance at where her phone might've landed— though she couldn't see it in the dim light—and she opted not to search for it. Better to take the offensive approach and deal with the intruder.

There'd be nowhere to seek shelter.

No place to hide.

The house had grown eerily quiet. The intruder's telltale light no longer revealed his presence.

Had the sound of her phone falling scared him away?

Shaylee sucked in a fortifying breath. Taking the last step from cover, she flattened herself against the wall and peered down the dark hallway. Silent seconds ticked by as she monitored the doorways of the other bedrooms and bathroom for any movement.

Not a sound and no sign of the intruder.

She slipped out of her bedroom, slithering along the hall, gun tightly gripped. Approaching the room on her right, Shaylee scanned the space sparsely furnished with a desk pushed to the far side beneath the window. She moved to the next bedroom and peered inside. Only the centered double bed and small dresser occupied the room.

Pausing at the end of the hallway, she saw the glow from the streetlamp outside cast shadows across the hardwood floors. Her eyes swept the living room, and immediately spotted what had awakened her. Several books lay scattered on the floor beside the jolted bookshelf.

Shaylee's throat tightened, threatening to cut off her oxygen supply. She crept from the safety of the hallway and started to pivot toward the kitchen.

Two quick hits, one to the side of her face, the other to her arm sent Shaylee stumbling back and her gun flying from her grip.

She caught herself before she fell, and prepared to strike.

Blinded by a bright light, Shaylee quickly averted her eyes. Spots danced before them. With a rush and a growl, the person tackled her, and she landed hard, slamming her head.

In a flash, the man pinned her down, bearing down his full weight on her torso. The flashlight hit the floor and rolled away.

Shaylee struggled to inhale.

Before she could shift her legs to gain position, he dug his knees into her forearms, locking them at her sides. She fought, twisting until he pressed something cold against her throat.

"Keep moving, and you'll cut your own neck."

"What do you want?" she gasped, frozen in place.

She searched the darkness, trying to focus on his face. He pushed the object harder against her skin, and a sharp sting indicated he'd nicked her with the blade. "I see Baxter still hides behind hired thugs to do his dirty work," she taunted.

"No loose ends." His voice was unfamiliar, and the black balaclava hood covered everything except his cold, dark eyes.

The man's weight hindered her breathing.

She refused to be rendered unconscious again. It was now or never.

If she miscalculated the next move, she would certainly slice her own throat.

Lord, give me strength. Shaylee bent her legs and thrust up her hips, throwing off the intruder. He rocked to the side, landing on one knee.

She shifted into a ground defense position, sliding to her left side and using her right foot to kick. She made contact with his upper torso, and he crashed onto his backside.

The knife clattered to the floor.

He stretched, reaching for it, and gave Shaylee precious seconds to scurry back on her hands and knees.

She jumped to her feet, and with palms facing her, one foot slightly in front of the other, she prepared to fight.

"You're going to pay for that." He stood opposite her.

Shaylee inched toward the door and the antique iron umbrella rack in the corner. Not the best weapon, but it would have to suffice.

He stalked her, sliding from side to side, taunting. Let him waste his energy. She watched, ready to pounce at the right moment.

A glimmer from the streetlamp flickered off the blade.

The very long blade.

She caught sight of her Colt lying to the side of the bookcase. All she needed was a distraction to grab it.

Shaylee lunged for the umbrella stand and hoisted it over her shoulders. With a battle cry, she charged the intruder and hurled the makeshift weapon. He turned, and the stand crashed into his back.

She dove for her Colt, snatching it off the floor.

He barreled through the kitchen and out the ajar door, jerking it closed behind him.

Shaylee gave chase, yanked the door open, and ran outside.

With no sight of the man, she rushed to the chain-link fence, searching her neighbors' yards.

The man had vanished into the night. She returned to the house replaying what he'd said. *No loose ends.* He hadn't asked for anything so clearly; he'd been determined to kill her.

Unless…

Shaylee ran to the bookshelf. *No. No.*

Zia's Bible lay on the table where she'd left it and the page from the accounting journal was gone.

TEN

Sunlight pierced the window and stabbed Jamey's throbbing skull. He groaned, struggling to shield himself with his pillow. The venture through the mountains had done a number on his arms and legs. Exhaustion immobilized him.

Just a few minutes more.

Must. Have. Coffee.

Why was it so hard to wake up? He wasn't that out of shape.

With one eyeball peering from beneath the covers, he spotted his phone on the nightstand and dragged the device as though it weighed a hundred pounds. He positioned it upright and stared at the time. 7:00 a.m.

The girls hadn't been out since the night before, and Echo would certainly need a potty break. Bugsy pressed against his legs, still snoring. Where was Echo?

Jamey used his leg, sliding it across the bed in search of the puppy.

Ugh, had she found some place in the room to do her business? Had she hopped down? That was a bit of a launch for her little body. Especially with a wounded appendage. "Echo?" Jamey's voice cracked. Shoving off the blankets, he sat up.

The world spun, and he gripped the sheets to ground himself.

Bugsy lay sprawled beside him, completely oblivious. Poor dog, she needed a break. But not today. They had to return to the sinkholes and search for Zia.

"Echo? Here, girl." His dry mouth prevented a whistle, so he stretched over the side to peer underneath and searched the floor. Pressing his fingers against the carpet, he stilled the spinning world.

He pushed up to a sitting position and caught sight of a tiny bundle near the foot of the bed. Jamey tugged off the blankets, revealing Echo's sleeping form. He reached and lifted her. Why wasn't she waking?

He glanced again at Bugsy.

Instinct rattled him.

Something was wrong.

"Come on, Bugsy, time to get up."

She didn't respond.

Her torso rose and fell steadily.

Jamey rubbed her side. "You had a rough day yesterday, but we gotta get moving. Come on, Bugs. You're in worse shape than I am," he teased.

She didn't move.

Worry constricted his throat. "Bugsy." He shook her body. Nothing.

Jamey snatched his cell phone off the bed and called the first person who came to mind.

Shaylee answered immediately, "I was just about to call you. I had—"

"The girls won't wake up. Can you drive us to Dr. Keough's?"

"I'm on my way. They're both still breathing?"

"Yes."

Movement in the background, and the sound of an engine coming to life filtered through the line. "Your voice sounds funny."

Jamey blinked, trying to clear his vision. "Something isn't right."

"What do you mean?"

"Everything is all blurry and my head is raging."

Shaylee gasped. "Get out of the house now! Call 911. Tell them you have a possible carbon monoxide leak. My ETA is five minutes."

"Okay." Jamey immediately dialed 911 and threw on a pair of jeans, then transported both dogs to the front yard. He settled them in the dew-covered grass and called Dr. Keough's emergency line. When he explained the symptoms and Shaylee's assumption, Dr. Keough agreed. "Do they have a pulse?"

"Yes."

"Get them here ASAP."

"I'm waiting on my ride. We should be there soon."

"Make sure they're outside, they need fresh air. I'll be waiting for you."

Jamey disconnected, praying Shaylee got there quickly.

Sirens cued in the distance.

Bugsy shifted slightly, her torso rising and falling. One eyeball opened weakly, then closed again. "Come on, girl. Breathe."

The sight of Shaylee's car brought a spark of relief. She parked and ran to him. "I blew the doors off the fire truck, passing them. You need to have the paramedics examine you."

"No time!"

Her gaze reverted to the unconscious dogs. "Car's running, let's go!"

They loaded the girls just as the fire department arrived, sirens screaming.

Jamey explained the details to the first firefighter he spotted.

"You say they won't wake up?" The man leaned to the side and peered into Shaylee's car.

"No. Shaylee thinks it might be carbon monoxide poisoning. But we have to get to the vet immediately."

"Paramedics should clear you."

"I'm fine. Really," Jamey insisted.

The firefighter nodded. "Understood. We'll need to air out the house and investigate for a leak."

"Do whatever you have to." Jamey slid into the passenger seat and hollered, "Shaylee, we have to go now!"

She said something to the crew, then joined Jamey and headed to the highway.

"I asked him to call you with an update."

"Thank you." He could hardly speak over the skull-splitting headache. "Please." Jamey's one-word prayer held his fears, hopes and request.

Shaylee grabbed his hand, joining him in the pleas for mercy and help.

When they reached the vet's office, Shaylee hadn't finished parking before Jamey thrust open the door and pulled out Bugsy. Shaylee carried Echo, and they hurried through the doors.

Dr. Keough took Bugsy from Jamey's arms. One of the vet assistants gathered Echo and rushed through the double doors.

Jamey started to follow, but a third assistant blocked him from entering and firmly placed a hand out to stop him. "I'm sorry, but you can't come back. We'll advise you if there is any change."

Shaylee was at his side, eyes shimmering. "C'mon, Jamey, let's sit over there."

He blinked, processing her words, then numbly trailed

behind her. A large fifty-five-gallon fish tank positioned against the wall provided him something to stare at.

His phone buzzed in his pocket, but he ignored the call. Nothing else mattered. Had his ambitions killed Bugsy? Guilt overwhelmed Jamey. What had he done? For Baxter to go after him was one thing, but the girls didn't deserve this.

He bowed his head. Sorrow and fear mingled with worry.

Shaylee's cell rang, and he vaguely overheard the conversation, "Hi, Chief. Yes, sorry, he's stressed. It did? Thanks."

Jamey studied her. The conversation was short and unrevealing. "Tests confirm your house had high levels of carbon monoxide. If you hadn't left when you did—" She didn't finish the sentence. She didn't need to.

Jamey's gaze returned to the double doors. Why wasn't anyone coming out to give them an update?

Shaylee squeezed his hand.

"This is ridiculous. The killer used carbon monoxide to poison us?"

"I want to say it's a coincidence, but I don't believe that. I'd hoped you'd be safe once we parted, Jamey."

He swallowed hard, searching for a comment, but nothing came to mind.

There was no safe place anymore.

If the killer invaded his home and created the leak, he couldn't return there with the dogs.

Bugsy and Echo were innocent.

They would be fine.

They had to be.

Jamey paced Dr. Keough's waiting room, grateful for Shaylee's company but unable to speak. Worry for Bugsy and Echo overrode everything else in his mind. He appreciated Shaylee's quiet support as he prayed, worried and waited.

Finally, the door opened and Dr. Keough stepped out, forehead creased with concern.

"Dr. Keough, are they okay?" Jamey rushed toward her and Shaylee moved to his side.

The veterinarian blew out a breath. "Yes. It's a good thing you got to them as fast as you did. They're in recovery and responding very well to treatment."

Jamey exhaled relief. "Thank you."

Because of her short stature, Dr. Keough had to stretch to place a calloused hand that spoke of age and hard work on his shoulder. "They'll be fine. I'd like to maintain steady oxygen for twenty-four hours to flush the toxins out of their systems. I'll call when they're ready to go."

Emotion thickened his throat, and he nodded. Would they be safe here, though? Would the killer return? "Is there any way we can take them home sooner? Please?"

Dr. Keough frowned. "I wouldn't recommend that, but we'll monitor their progress, and if possible, I'll release them."

"Dr. Keough, would you be so kind as to send an update in an hour? I understand that's a lot to ask," Shaylee interceded.

"Not a problem. I'll text you. It's serious, I won't tell you otherwise. However, I'm optimistic." She smiled kindly.

"Can I see them before we go?" Jamey asked.

"Of course." Dr. Keough led Jamey and Shaylee through the double doors and into the recovery room where both dogs lay asleep in steel kennels. IV bags hung outside the doors, and oxygen masks were strapped over their muzzles. "Don't let their appearance scare you. We had to sedate them to keep them from pulling out the IVs."

Jamey dropped to his knees, and Dr. Keough opened Bugsy's kennel door. He knelt beside her and stroked her soft ears. Tears blurred his vision at the sight of his precious friend lying helpless. "Get well fast," he whispered, not caring who heard him.

Shaylee cooed softly to Echo.

"I'll text you when they wake," Dr. Keough promised.

Jamey pushed to stand and swallowed the sadness. He and Shaylee exited the veterinarian's office wordlessly, stepping out to the warm spring afternoon. He slid into the passenger seat.

Numbness consumed him.

Shaylee started the car. "Why don't we grab breakfast? The fire department is airing out your place, and Captain Dugan promised to secure the house. Once Dr. Keough releases the dogs, we can head back. They should've cleared the scene by then."

Jamey shook his head. "I'm not taking the girls to my house. Who knows what else this maniac will do? And I don't want to leave them unattended at the vet. I cannot endanger them again." Frustration, helplessness and fury at his inability to fix the situation had Jamey flustered. "Why would someone do something so cruel? Kill me, fine, but don't hurt the animals. They have nothing to do with you or me. It's unconscionable."

"Jamey, this is my fault. I never should've involved you in my mess. I can't tell you how sorry I am."

"This isn't on you." He ran a hand through his hair. "Why use a carbon monoxide leak? There are much faster methods."

"Baxter is relentless, though, and making your death look like an accident would be his MO. He obviously sees the threat you pose."

"Which is why he'd want to eliminate Bugsy, too. She's the one with the superpower to find Zia," Jamey concluded.

"Exactly."

"Even if I walked away from the investigation, he'd still come after me."

"I agree."

Shaylee parked in front of a small café. "Let's go inside. I need to talk to you."

The bell chimed over the restaurant door, announcing their arrival.

"Sit wherever you like." The fortysomething woman waved them inside. She wore a plaid shirt and jeans, and her blond hair was pulled into a high ponytail.

Shaylee chose a corner booth in the back. The server took their order and poured coffee, then stepped away.

Jamey circled the cup with his hands. "Thank you for coming to our rescue this morning. You were the first person I thought of."

"Honestly, I was waiting to call you."

He met her eyes.

Shaylee blew out a breath. "I need to apologize. After the way we parted yesterday, I wasn't sure you'd want to talk to me."

"You don't owe me anything. I'm the one who needs to apologize."

She tilted her head in confusion. "Why would you think that?"

"I was a jerk. You have no reason to trust me. I'm not privy to the case files. I shouldn't have assumed I deserved to be included in the investigation. But I would really like to help, in whatever capacity it's acceptable."

"I'm glad you said that because I was unsure who else to turn to." Shaylee's eyes shimmered, and she looked away.

"Why? Did something happen?"

"Sorry, I'm tired, and my emotions are a little raw. Honestly, I would've called you at three o'clock, but I was dealing with crime scene techs and Captain Dugan."

"Wait, did you say crime scene techs?"

She slipped off her jacket, placing it beside her in the booth, and turned to face him. Frowning, she placed a finger against her lips, drawing his attention to the abrasion on her neck.

He leaned forward. "Shaylee, what happened? Who did that to you?" Concern for her consumed him.

"It's a long story. You'll need coffee first."

Jamey sipped and gave her the space she needed to continue. He listened as Shaylee told him about the intruder in her home. "Someone broke in? Again? You have to get out of there."

"I should install an alarm system. Maybe once Echo recovers she could move in with me, or is she too young to be a guard dog?" Her laugh sounded forced, as though she was half-joking, half-serious.

"Dogs deter burglars. She won't understand attacking on command, but she'll alert you to an unwelcome presence," Jamey agreed.

"A little warning would've done wonders." Shaylee took a sip.

The server returned with their breakfasts, sliding overflowing plates in front of them. "Holler at me if you want anything else."

"Thank you, ma'am," Jamey replied.

She smiled and moved to the counter to assist a new arrival.

Shaylee continued, "I surprised the intruder by waking up while he was helping himself to my house. That's when he attacked me." She gestured to the cut. "And we discovered he didn't break in. He used my spare key and left it stuck in the lock."

Jamey considered her words, processing the implication. "How did he know where to find your key? Did you get a good look at him?" He sucked in a breath. "Sorry,

I—" He again raked a hand through his hair. "Let's start over. Are you all right?"

"Yeah. I'm angry more than anything. And to answer your question, I keep a spare in a fake rock by the door."

"But your neck." He wanted to go to her, to pull her into his arms, but he worked on separating the strips of bacon on his plate instead.

She fingered the injury. "Just a scrape. Definitely could've been worse. And no, I can't identify him thanks to the classic black balaclava he wore." She lifted a piece of toast and took a bite. "Anyway, that's the reason our department crime scene tech is working at my house, but I doubt she'll find anything. And I have a bigger problem."

"Bigger than almost dying?"

"The intruder stole that page of the accounting journal. Jamey, I was so stupid. I thought I'd hidden it in Zia's Bible on my bookshelf, but I left it sitting on my coffee table after Noreen came by."

"Noreen Liddle?" Jamey remembered Baxter's mousy intern from the trial.

"Yeah, she stopped to check on me."

Convenient. He'd never even met the woman, but she comprised part of Baxter's coterie, and he wanted nothing to do with her. "How did she know what had happened to you?"

Shaylee rolled her eyes. "She says Franny told her."

Jamey quirked a brow. "What? That should've been confidential."

"No matter, Franny knows we're close." Shaylee waved his comment away. "Besides, are you kidding? In this town? After Dugan brought in Franny on the situation and the firefighters and rescue workers looked for the coffin, I'm sure the news spread faster than the flames they battled."

"Did Dugan release your identity as the victim?"

"No, but it wouldn't take much to find that out."

Jamey nodded. He understood the fuel of juicy gossip, especially something as bizarre as a woman buried alive in the mountains. Like getting a two-by-four upside the head, he realized Shaylee had involved Noreen by showing her the journal. The one she hadn't willingly offered to him. "You showed the evidence to Baxter's intern?"

Shaylee winced. "It sounds bad, but she has access to Baxter's financials, and she promised to do some digging."

"And why would she do that?"

Shaylee circled the top of her coffee cup with a finger. "Noreen is the most devoted person you'd ever meet."

Jamey rubbed the stubble on his chin. "Great. So she's going to run and tell him everything and then what?"

"Actually, the opposite. She's been a family friend since we were kids. Zia and I babysat her. She'd never hurt me. And she really thinks the world of Baxter. She wants him proven innocent. She made me promise that if I don't find anything implicating him, I will let it go."

Jamey gaped at her. "Tell me you're joking?"

"Nope." She gave him a conspiratorial grin. "But you and I both know he's guilty. So that's not an issue."

Speechless, he waited for Shaylee to continue.

"Anyway, I'm thrilled she agreed to help me. But after she left, exhaustion won out. I crashed, and forgot about hiding the page. It was right there on the coffee table, practically shouting, 'Hey, steal me.' And since I went blasting into Baxter's house, swinging the document in his face, he knew exactly what to look for. How could I have been so careless? That was the only new clue I had. And it's gone." Shaylee looked down, pushing her food around on her plate.

"Maybe it's not as bad as it seems."

She grunted. "I appreciate your optimism, but I don't think there's any way to save this."

"I'm sorry." Still, it didn't explain why she'd suddenly chosen to involve him.

Clearly, protection detail wasn't his forte.

He focused on her. Why hadn't he pushed to see it? He'd allowed his pride to interfere yesterday. He refused to go down that road. She was here, face-to-face with him. That said something, right? If she didn't trust him, she wouldn't have bothered. But he had to know. "I'm curious why you hesitated to show me the journal."

"Jamey, I failed to save Zia, and that haunts me every single day. I didn't want to drag anyone else into my nightmare. Look at yesterday. I put you and Bugsy in danger multiple times. I thought by not involving you further, I'd protect you."

"Well now that we know this guy is out to kill both of us, parting ways is unwise. Strength in numbers and all that. If you trust me to partner with you on this case." He searched her eyes, hopeful.

"If you hadn't called me this morning, I had planned to call you. And without a doubt, I trust you with my life. You've more than proven yourself capable. I thought I could handle it on my own. But after last night, I realized I have no one else to turn to right now."

Her confession warmed his heart. "You have an entire police force."

"Actually, I don't. And I've lost the only lead I had."

"They have to investigate Baxter before something horrible happens to you." He considered his words. "I mean, not to undermine the terror of being buried alive and attacked in a home invasion, but I think you're right. Baxter will kill you and anyone else involved."

ELEVEN

Shaylee blinked. "You agree with me about Baxter?"

Jamey tilted his head as though she'd spoken the words in a foreign language. "Um, yeah."

The lonely battle she'd fought since Zia's disappearance had taken a toll, and gratitude swelled from within, his affirmation soothing her.

A text message from Noreen chimed, interrupting their discussion.

Need to talk. Your house?

Shaylee responded. Unsafe. Pick a place.

McCade Park, south shelter, 7:30

"Noreen wants to meet," she explained.

Jamey sat up straighter. "Great. I'll go with you."

Appreciation for his willingness warred with her independence. And knowing Noreen, she couldn't risk scaring her off when they were so close. "She's paranoid about Baxter finding out. I'll go alone."

"That's not wise."

Shaylee sighed. "It'll be okay. I'll keep my phone close."

"Why not call instead of text?" Jamey asked, taking a bite of bacon.

"Probably hard to talk since she's around Baxter twenty-four seven. I'm sure she's keeping the communication on the down-low."

Jamey snorted.

Shaylee's cell phone rang again. "Wow, I'm popular this morning. Oh, it's Captain Dugan."

"How're the dogs?" Dugan blurted in greeting.

"Dr. Keough says they'll recover, but she's monitoring them for a while."

"I'm glad to hear that. Firefighters released Jamey's house, but Adler, there's a problem."

"It's becoming my life, sir. I'm afraid to ask for clarification."

"I just received a call from Baxter's legal counsel. They've warned they will file a motion naming you, me and anyone else in the department if you continue 'slandering' Baxter."

Shaylee clenched her hands. "Seriously? They're calling it *slander*? Threatening us for doing our jobs?"

"After your visit to his house and the subsequent events, apparently it's caused talk among his constituents and he's concerned about his reputation and public image. You knocked him off his pedestal, kiddo."

"Good." Shaylee leaned back against the booth seat.

"I've got your back. But without solid evidence, your investigation and outspoken nature will sink us both. We'll be typing our résumés. And in case you hadn't noticed, I'm too old to start over. I'm looking forward to retirement in the next few years, not an entry-level job where I get a fresh start in a new career."

The weight of his words fell on her. "He's vindictive enough to do that."

"Yes, he is. I'm guessing Jamey can attest to Baxter's reach."

Shaylee lowered her voice. "Sir, regardless of whether I investigate or not, Jamey, the dogs and I remain on Baxter's kill list. His culprit stole the journal, but that doesn't mean the attacks will stop."

"I agree. Here's the catch. I cannot allow you to investigate Baxter on the clock. It's too risky to us both."

She huffed. "I've had more attempts on my life in the past forty-eight hours than my entire career. I will take down Baxter with or without your permission."

"Let's try that again because we're clearly not communicating." Dugan's warning hung in the air. "You're a grown woman, Detective Adler, and I cannot control what you do on your time. But you cannot utilize department resources and I will not authorize additional personnel to assist in your investigation of Baxter Heathcote."

Shaylee gritted her teeth, then processed his words, absorbing the hidden meaning. "Roger that. Then, sir, I respectfully request a few personal days to deal with these most recent events."

"Granted." Dugan lowered his voice. "In all seriousness, Adler, I want Baxter behind bars as much as you. Nothing would bring me more joy. I'm sick of his bullying and threats. The only way to successfully do that is by using our brains. You cannot threaten Baxter again. Communicate only with me. If and/or when you find evidence implicating him, you will contact me first. Do not, I repeat, do not, notify anyone else. Understood?"

"Yes, sir. Jamey and the dogs are in danger, too."

"The incident could've resulted from a carbon monoxide leak on an old appliance."

"Do you really believe that?"

Dugan sighed. "No."

"We have to find Zia and end this."

"Agreed, and I hate that it's the only option. I've reprimanded the officer who failed on your security assignment last night. There was a false report of an armed robbery that took him away."

"Baxter," Shaylee muttered.

"Probably. As long as he sees you both as a threat, he won't stop until you're dead. Detective Greer is working the attacks against you. However, I've told him nothing about Baxter. Understood?"

"Affirmative." Greer would record the melted coffin and break-in without specifically naming Baxter. "Thank you."

"Keep me apprised."

"Roger that." They disconnected.

Shaylee updated Jamey on the conversation. "My day keeps getting better. Captain Dugan agrees the attacks are connected to Zia's case, but without evidence specifically pointing to Baxter, he can't authorize an official investigation. We're a small-town department and there's not enough personnel. And Baxter's threatening legal recourse if I continue 'slandering' him." She made air quotes with her fingers.

"Aren't the attacks enough?"

"They're proof someone wants me dead. Just not enough to prove who. Dugan's assigned an investigator and I'm taking leave time. It'll allow me to work the case under the wire without explaining my time or activities."

"Interpretation, you're on your own. Otherwise, if you fail and Baxter gets wind of the investigation, you all lose your jobs?" Jamey clarified.

"You got it." Shaylee chomped on a piece of bacon.

"Been there, done that," Jamey mumbled. "Baxter's nothing if not consistent. If he doesn't kill you, he'll find other ways to ruin you, professionally and personally."

"I'd say we've already started that hourglass. Either way, I will take down Baxter."

Jamey poked at the food on his plate. "Baxter destroyed my reputation with law enforcement, but Bugsy and I are a great team. Our previous cases are proof. I'll continue my search for Zia, regardless. It's not as if I'm worried about losing my job." He snorted. "Baxter already took care of that."

"Finding her might restore your job and your reputation. It would prove you were right all along." Shaylee sighed. "Asking you to risk your life isn't fair. You should take the dogs and go somewhere safe."

Jamey shook his head. "No way. You're not doing this alone. Baxter's got long arms, but he's not invincible."

"If we fail to find Zia, he'll come after you, too."

"I have nothing else to lose. Don't get me wrong, I do dread starting over again, should it come down to that. Going from the lab to the classroom wasn't anything I had planned. But God always provides. I fear God more than I fear Baxter's wrath. And—" Jamey hesitated, and Shaylee searched his blue eyes.

"Are you sure you want to do this? We're both fully aware of the repercussions. How can I ask you to sacrifice your own life for what might be the ultimate destruction of all you've built?"

Jamey reached across the table and took her hand, enveloping it in his own. "We haven't known each other long, but I will not stand by and do nothing. I'm in this with you. I'll fight beside you. For you. Whatever it takes. I'm fully aware of the cost. And I'm willing to pay it, for you."

He squeezed her hand reassuringly, and Shaylee's heart felt like it would burst in her chest. She studied him, lost in the depths of the man before her. What made up Jamey Dyer? This honorable guy who'd promised to sacrifice everything to help her.

In that moment, Shaylee knew nothing would ever be the same between them.

No matter what happened, Jamey Dyer was the hero she'd searched for her whole life.

Their gazes locked, and Shaylee sucked in a breath.

The table separated them, but if it didn't, would he kiss her?

Her phone rang, and she reluctantly released Jamey's hand. "Captain Dugan again. Yes, sir?"

"With both your homes compromised, you need a neutral and secret location."

"I agree."

"Do I need to find you a safe house?"

An idea sprouted. "Actually, Noreen's grandmother owned a cabin in the mountains. It's vacant, and Noreen never goes there."

"Would you have to notify her you were using it?" Dugan asked.

"Not at all. Before Zia passed, Noreen allowed us to use it whenever we wanted without notice. I haven't been there since…but I know it's not a problem."

"Then do it. But tell no one, including Noreen. Understand?"

"Roger that."

"Call me if you need anything."

"Thanks, Captain."

They disconnected again.

She glanced up at Jamey, who was watching her with interest. "How do you feel about moving?"

Jamey raised his eyebrows, trying to comprehend Shaylee's suggestion about using a cabin Noreen Liddle owned. "Nothing like sleeping in the lion's den."

"I'm telling you Noreen isn't like that. She never goes

there anymore. The place stays vacant. A little run-down but off the grid."

Jamey sighed. "If I had a better idea, I'd argue, but I don't." At least they would be together, and he could protect Shaylee.

A text from Dr. Keough said the girls were doing well and could leave earlier than anticipated. They hurried to finish their meal, and he paid the bill.

Jamey couldn't get to Bugsy fast enough, and he appreciated Shaylee's shared excitement.

They hurried through the vet's doors to Dr. Keough, who greeted them with a smile. "Two very energetic ladies are waiting for you."

The assistant went inside and returned with both dogs leashed. At the sight of Bugsy, Jamey held out his arms, and she jumped into them, licking his face. Echo barked, bouncing at his feet. Shaylee lifted her, relishing the puppy's affection.

Dr. Keough gave them instructions. "Jamey, you have my cell number. If you see anything of concern, call me. No matter what time." She gave him a new prescription for Echo.

"I will." Jamey purchased new food for both dogs, not wanting to risk them eating food tainted with carbon monoxide, and they loaded the girls into Shaylee's car, then slid into their seats.

Shaylee glanced at him and smiled. "I think I'm in love."

He blinked. Did she mean him? "Um—"

"I know she's yours, but, Jamey, I'd really love to adopt Echo."

He swallowed. Shaylee meant the dog. Unsure whether he was relieved or disappointed he exhaled, grateful he hadn't spoken his confusion. "I think that's a great idea. On one condition."

"Name it."

"You allow me to help train you together. She's got the potential to do great things, especially in search and rescue." And it would give him a reason to see Shaylee.

"Can I tell you a secret?"

His heart thrummed. "Please do."

She leaned over and whispered, "I have always wanted to work with a SAR dog. I would absolutely love that." Shaylee's breath warm against his ear sent a shiver through him. "Let's hit my place first. It's on the edge of town and then we can head to the cabin."

Clearing his throat, he croaked, "Sounds good." Jamey spent the majority of the drive regaining control over his senses.

Shaylee pulled up to a small bungalow and parked in the driveway. "Come on in."

Jamey unloaded the dogs, giving them a potty break, then followed Shaylee inside. Black powder from the fingerprinting materials marred the walls and counters. An umbrella rack lay on the floor against one wall. Leaving the place in such disarray nagged at Jamey's conscience, but they couldn't linger.

"I'll only be a minute." Shaylee disappeared down the hall.

Jamey moseyed around the living room, glancing at the books on Shaylee's shelf, and Bugsy pawed at something near the couch.

"Hey, girl, what'd you find?" He knelt and peered underneath, spotting a jagged white object.

"I appreciate your preference for cleanliness but checking for dust bunnies under my furniture is a little excessive," Shaylee said, returning to the living room.

Jamey sat back on his heels. "Bugsy clawed at the floor. I'm not sure what she found, but I don't want to just tug it out. Do you have a plastic glove or something I can grab this with?"

Shaylee walked to the closet and withdrew latex gloves from a duffel bag.

They donned the gloves, and Jamey retrieved the object. "It almost looks like polished bone or stone. Based on the jagged edges, I'd surmise it broke off something." He passed it to Shaylee. "Look familiar?"

She turned the item over, holding it up to the light. "Actually, it does, but I can't place where I've seen this before."

"Maybe a clue left behind by your attacker?"

"Possibly? It's familiar. I'll send a picture to Captain Dugan to keep him in the loop. We can't stay here long, and I don't want the evidence collector to make another mess." She took a quick picture with her cell phone.

Jamey bagged the object and dropped it into his pocket.

Shaylee grabbed her bag, and they headed out. The drive was quick to his place, and he immediately spotted his pickup in the driveway. "At least my truck is finished."

"Having two vehicles might be a good thing," Shaylee said.

"I'll load the girls, and we'll follow you to the cabin. Give me two minutes."

Shaylee led the dogs to the backyard, and Jamey sped through the house. Nothing appeared out of order until he inspected the water heater. Telltale indicators of the brownish-yellow stains around the base showed where the carbon monoxide had leaked into the house, confirming the firefighters' assessment.

Jamey gathered his backpack and hiking equipment, then walked out to the yard, where Shaylee sat under the large elm tree.

"I guess I'll be buying a new water heater." He explained the findings. "Although I'm certain there was nothing wrong with it a few days ago."

"Undoubtedly."

Sharp piercing barks rang out from the corner of the yard where Bugsy and Echo stood focused on an object. Jamey spotted something shiny and hurried over. He snatched the wrapper off the ground, then inspected both dogs, assuring they hadn't ingested any of the chocolate. Satisfied, he gave them head rubs and praise. "Good job, Bugsy!"

"What was that all about?"

"This." Jamey held out the ripped chocolate wrapper.

"Chocolate?"

"Yeah. It's lethal for dogs. Thankfully, I think I got to it before they swallowed any. Three trips to Dr. Keough in two days might have the humane society after me." He sighed.

Shaylee looked around the yard. "Where did it come from? I guess one of the rescue workers could've dropped it."

"If only I thought that was the case." He inspected the white paper tinted with green splotches. "Antifreeze."

"What?"

"Someone planted that for the dogs to find." Fury raged through him.

"Before the carbon monoxide poisoning?"

"Or last night. Anything's possible." He stormed to the house and grabbed a plastic bag and sealed the candy inside to deliver to the crime scene investigator.

The incident solidified what he'd already concluded. They couldn't stay here.

And the need to find the killer was gaining speed.

TWELVE

"It's a little in need of work," Shaylee explained, silently second-guessing her idea to stay in the Liddle cabin.

Shaylee and Jamey stood beside their vehicles parked beneath a canopy of trees and surveyed the property surrounding the two-bedroom log structure. The overgrown yard bordering the Black Hills Forest loomed wide, with thickets and bushes reaching out like arms reclaiming the land.

The gravel driveway lined by towering trees wound half a mile from the rural road before dead-ending at the run-down structure. Massive pines concealed their presence from passersby, though the rustic location didn't appear to get much traffic.

A definite positive.

The unkempt premises, with the wild grass in desperate need of mowing, forced Shaylee to high-step to the door. Wildflowers sprouted up in random areas with tiny bursts of color among the yellowing ground. In her peripheral vision she spotted Jamey and the dogs meandering across the property.

She made her way to the rickety swing on the decaying porch and retrieved the brass key hidden under the wooden slats. "Aha!"

At her declaration, Jamey approached. "Eureka?"

"Yep." She walked to the door and inserted the key into the lock.

"Does everyone hide spare house keys?"

She chuckled. "I guess it's a Midwest thing. Although I will hide mine better in the future." She unlocked the door and pushed it wide.

Musty air and dust greeted them, and the darkened cabin appeared ominous with the drapes closed. Shaylee moved to each window, parting the curtains to allow natural light to enter.

Shaylee provided a mini tour, gesturing as she spoke. "Kitchenette, dining room, living room." She moved to the far side and pointed to the narrow hallway. "Bedroom at the end and a compact bathroom on the right. To the left, stairs lead to the loft bedroom."

Jamey and the dogs roamed the main floor. He walked to the stairs and his heavy footfalls sounded on the wooden slats overhead.

Based on the layer of undisturbed dust, Noreen hadn't returned to the cabin in months. Not unusual. She hated the place, though Shaylee never understood why.

Shaylee opened the refrigerator, unsurprised at the emptiness except for a box of baking soda that had seen better days. She removed and tossed it into the trash. Good thing they'd stopped for groceries before their arrival.

Jamey pulled out a chair at the round oak table and sat. "Rustic definitely describes this place." He swiped the single countertop with his finger and frowned.

"Noreen never liked being out here. Zia and I used this place for girls' weekend getaways." She glanced at the table, where a single drop of red nail polish testified to their mani-pedi sessions. "I haven't been back since losing Zia."

The joyous memories of watching romantic comedies, on the old TV and VCR while eating vast amounts of brownies and sharing secrets tightened her chest with emotion. "I'll get the supplies."

Jamey followed her. "Those can wait. Let the inside air out a bit. Show me around while we still have daylight."

"Good idea." They walked the property, and the dogs followed. Echo disappeared in the tall grass, a black puff emerging occasionally as she bounded. "It's beautiful."

"I might have to consider moving out here," Jamey said.

Bugsy barked, chasing and playing with Echo.

"There are probably so many unfamiliar scents for them," Shaylee assessed.

"Definitely." They made their way to the small picnic table.

"Let's talk about the case and establish our game plan."

"We can safely assume the killer is familiar with the area where he buried you. Let's pull up a map of Black Hills National Forest. We'll head out first thing in the morning."

"Do you think the dogs will be okay to make the trip with us?" Shaylee asked.

Echo barked, playfully nipping at Bugsy's feet and running around. Bugsy gave chase, and the two rolled in the grass.

"I'd recommend leaving Echo with Captain Dugan," Jamey replied.

Shaylee sighed. "I love having her with me, but she would be a liability at this point."

He nodded. "Assuming Baxter is the culprit, how does that fit in with Black Hills National Forest?"

Shaylee pressed a finger to her lips. "Hmm. What if it's not his personal connection, but the person working for him? Probably a local?"

"Possibly. Or like this place, somewhere he's vacationed before?"

Shaylee frowned. "It's not like we can go to every hotel

and resort nearby and ask, 'Hey, seen any coffin-toting killers around here?' There are tons of little cabins like this sprinkled all over the forest, as well."

Jamey chuckled. "Imagine the looks we'd get."

"Right?" She gave him a crooked grin.

Jamey waved at a mosquito.

"Sorry, the bugs are out of control here."

"We're in their domain. They're just looking for dinner." Jamey and Shaylee walked to the porch swing and swayed gently. "So, our killer drives a truck or large SUV big enough to transport the coffin and a UTV. There's no way he carried the coffin into the mountains. And most likely, he was aware the sinkholes had closed the area to the public, which gave him an advantage. He had knowledge of inconspicuous places. He entered the park without being detected by the guards at the main entrances."

Shaylee considered his assessment. "Definitely a local. Baxter owns an SUV, as you're aware."

Jamey grunted.

"I'm not sure about the UTV. He's not really the outdoorsy type, but Noreen can answer that for sure. If he hired someone, that's a whole different story."

"Working with a partner is risky, though," Jamey contended.

Shaylee hunched over, hugging her calves. "Ugh! I don't want to talk myself out of going after Baxter."

Jamey touched her back, and she slowly sat up. "We're considering all the possibilities. I'm positive the gypsum mine is the key to finding Zia and identifying her killer."

Conflict etched in Jamey's expression and gave Shaylee pause. "What are you not saying?"

Jamey stood and paced, finally leaning against the closest tree. "I've never been overly confident, but before the trial, I trusted the science I'd presented."

"Having your testimony attacked left you doubting yourself," Shaylee surmised.

"Yes, but more than that. In the past, I helped victims by presenting strong scientific evidence. I put the smoking gun in the killer's hands, figuratively speaking."

Shaylee's heart melted at his tender confession. How many times had she relied on her training and skills to do her job? Having her expertise questioned would scar her confidence. "I understand why that would jolt you, but you're brilliant. I've seen you in action."

Jamey shrugged. "Whatever we find, it has to be indisputable because a jury might not believe me. I wanted to warn you."

Shaylee slid off the swing and closed the distance between them. "I believe in you."

Their gazes held for several seconds. Birds chirped overhead; the dogs playfully barked. A slight breeze fluttered a loose strand of her hair. Jamey gently tucked it behind her ear, grazing her face. He traced the contours of her jaw. His touch was gentle and strong. She closed her eyes, relishing the sensation.

Jamey leaned closer. His breath was warm, and the smell of peppermint lingered between them.

Shaylee's phone chimed with a text, and her eyes flew open.

Jamey stepped back, shoving his hands into his pockets.

"Sorry," Shaylee whispered, truly meaning the word. She glanced at the phone. Noreen.

I'm on my way.

"Oh, I lost track of time. I need to meet Noreen. I'd better go." Yet Shaylee didn't move.

Echo bounded to her side, playfully nipping at her pant leg.

"I think someone wants to ride along," Jamey said. "Might be good to have a watchdog with you."

Shaylee grinned and lifted the little pup. Echo lavished kisses on her face, eliciting a giggle. "You talked me into it."

Jamey set his jaw. "Shaylee, I am going with you."

"Noreen is skittish. She's got the insider information I need. I don't want to scare her off."

"I'll keep a distance."

"No. Please. Stay here. We can't risk the killer finding this place."

Jamey shook his head, then quirked a brow. "But if you go now, Bugsy and I might eat all the steak before you return."

"That's a cruel dilemma. I earned that steak crawling through those atrocious tunnels," she teased.

He shrugged. "If I go with you, we'll get back at the same time."

Bugsy whined.

"See, she agrees," he said.

Shaylee grinned, but didn't dismiss the conflict she saw warring within him. "I have to do this. Alone."

He sighed surrender. "Fine. Let me get a leash for Echo." Jamey rushed into the cabin and returned with the simple yellow leash Dr. Keough had provided. He expertly looped the cord, creating a temporary collar/leash combination.

"We have to find something more fashionable when this is over," Shaylee said.

"She'd probably appreciate that, but this will do so she doesn't run off on you. She's got a lot of puppy energy to burn."

"I'll be in touch." Shaylee hurried to her car, excitement building.

"Wait!" Jamey rushed to her side. "How will I know if you're okay? How long should this take? I mean, I need to know when to start the grill." His playful grin nearly undid her resolve.

Shaylee settled Echo in the passenger seat. "I'm not sure. Depends on what Noreen tells me. If I'm not back by nightfall, worry." She smiled and slid behind the wheel.

"That doesn't make me feel better."

"It'll be fine. It's only Noreen, and she's as harmless as they come."

She closed the door and eased off the property to the rural road, shoving away the doubt about going alone. No. This wouldn't take long. She scratched Echo's velvety ears. "We're going to be fine, right?"

She pulled into McCade Park with three minutes to spare. "We made good time," she announced.

Echo gazed up with dark, innocent eyes.

She surveyed the empty lot. No sign of Noreen's car. "Hmm, guess we beat her here?"

Shaylee exited her vehicle and carried the pup to the shelter. A white six-foot fence boarded one side where several picnic tables sat beneath a steel canopy on a concrete slab. As she rounded the fence, she spotted Noreen sitting in the shadows, out of sight.

"You're pretty good at this clandestine meeting thing. Consider leaving politics and join the PD."

Noreen pushed up her glasses, forehead creased. "My stomach can't take this kind of pressure." Catching sight of Echo, she smiled. "Aw, you brought the puppy."

Shaylee hoisted Echo higher for Noreen to see. "Meet Echo."

Noreen extended a hand. "I'd cuddle her in a minute if my skin wouldn't blow up with hives."

"Oops, forgot about that." Shaylee set Echo down, allowing her to explore the full length of her short leash. She slid onto the bench seat opposite Noreen.

Echo scratched her neck with her hind leg and resumed scouring the grounds.

Noreen smiled, but it never reached her eyes.

"You don't look well. Are you okay?"

Noreen swiped at the hair around her forehead, damp with perspiration. "I can't do this. I feel like the worst kind of traitor."

Shaylee's pulse increased with anticipation. After the day they'd had, she'd welcome good news. "Did you find anything?"

"Nope. I searched through the last two years of accounting records. Nothing out of the ordinary."

"Did you see pages that looked ripped?"

Noreen shook her head.

Shaylee sighed. Of course not, that would be too easy. "There's gotta be something in his files. Search his personal account, look for transfers?"

"Already did and nearly got fired over it. I don't want to lose my job. He's stressed with the swearing-in ceremony in a couple of days."

"I understand." And that upped her internal timer. They had to get him before he was sworn in. "Hey, does Baxter own a UTV or trailer?"

"No. Why do you ask?"

"I'm piecing things together."

"Since I found nothing, you'll back off the investigation, right?" Noreen's eyes moved quickly, surveying Shaylee.

"I'm not through."

"I know you hate Baxter, but, Shaylee, he didn't kill Zia. I'm absolutely positive he's innocent. Maybe Zia just left. I mean they found her car and she's never returned. It's a possibility. She hated the public life. People run away from their lives all the time."

Shaylee opened her mouth to speak, and Noreen interrupted with a lifted hand. "Hear me out. If you're focused on Baxter, you're doing a biased investigation. That's not ethical."

Shaylee swallowed and glanced down at her hands. Was Noreen right? Had her disdain for Baxter forced her to fit everything she found into the Baxter-shaped box she'd invented?

Noreen touched her shoulder. "Please walk away from this. Sometimes there aren't answers this side of eternity. Not everything gets wrapped with a neat bow. I'm not diminishing your pain or Zia's loss. But I hate seeing what this obsession is doing to you."

"What about the threats on my life? I can't ignore that. I didn't ask to be kidnapped and buried alive. I didn't ask the intruder to invade my home." Shaylee bit her lip, contemplating whether to tell Noreen about the carbon monoxide incident at Jamey's house. She decided against it.

Noreen sighed, withdrawing her hand. "I don't want you to get hurt."

Shaylee snorted. "It's a little late for that. But I understand you not wanting to be involved. It wasn't fair to ask you to help me. But I have to finish this." She told Noreen about the break-in and the loss of the journal page.

Noreen's eyes widened behind the large glasses. "Oh, Shaylee. See? You must quit. You're in danger."

"That's why I can't stop. If I don't find the killer, he won't give up until I'm dead. There's no place for me to go. I'm not safe in my own home."

Noreen nibbled on a fingernail. "There's no choice. I understand."

Shaylee reached out and touched her hand. "I was wrong to drag you into this mess. I can see what it's doing to you. So I officially release you from any more involvement." She forced levity into her tone.

"No. If you're involved, then so am I. I'll keep searching for clues. But where will you live?"

Shaylee glanced down, reminded she wasn't to share

their location. Yet they were staying in Noreen's grand-mother's cabin. Didn't she deserve to know that? Still, she couldn't compromise their only safe place. Hiding their location wasn't just about her protection. Jamey and the dogs relied on her. "Don't worry about me. I always land on my feet."

A chime drew Noreen's attention, and she glanced at her smartwatch. "I need to go. Baxter will wonder where I am." She rose.

Echo tugged and Shaylee released her hold, allowing the puppy to explore with the yellow leash trailing behind. She joined Noreen, keeping watch of Echo. "I didn't see your car."

"I parked down the road and walked."

"You really are good at clandestine work."

Noreen gave her a weak smile. Together they moved around the shelter. She turned to see Echo bounding away in pursuit of a gaggle of geese. Shaylee took a shortcut through the opposite side of the shelter. "Echo, no!"

A click sounded, and a blast launched Shaylee.

Her feet skimmed the grass as she flew through the air.

Heat and fire roared from the shelter.

Shaylee landed in a belly-flop position, thrusting the air from her lungs.

Grass poked her face.

With a groan, she pushed up and twisted around. Stunned by the inferno, she gaped. Noreen lay splayed facedown, a few feet away.

Echo scrambled to Shaylee, and she scooped up the dog.

Getting to her feet, she hurried to Noreen and gently rolled her over. "Noreen!"

Her friend's groan was a welcome sound.

Noreen opened her eyes. "What happened?" Abrasions marred the side of her face and her glasses, now broken, perched crookedly on her nose.

Shaylee helped her sit up. "Are you hurt?"

"No, I don't think so."

"Our killer apparently knew we were here. Who did you tell you were coming to meet me?"

"No one." Noreen frowned and glanced at her cell phone lying in the grass, screen shattered. "My phone. Did someone track me? Or yours?"

Shaylee considered that. Noreen's text message provided the location. "I'll call 911."

Noreen clamped a hand on her arm. "No! Please, Shaylee. No one can know I was here. Baxter will fire me."

Shaylee nodded. "Go. I'll handle the report."

"Please stop this madness. Someone is trying to kill you. Walk away. Take a vacation. Go somewhere safe."

"Don't you understand? There is no place safe. Not until I arrest this criminal! But you need to stay away from me. I don't want anything to happen to you."

Noreen got to her feet. "If you refuse, I will stay in the fight with you. Where are you staying? You could come to my house."

"I love you for offering, but you know that's not a possibility. Baxter would have a fit. I'll be fine. Go. Before the authorities get here." Shaylee hugged Noreen.

"But how will I reach you if I find anything?"

"Get a burner and send the number to my cell."

"Got it."

Shaylee lifted her phone and studied it. Was she being tracked? She dialed, watching Noreen disappear in the tree line.

"911, what's your emergency?"

If he didn't keep busy, Jamey would lose his mind. After Shaylee left, he put away the groceries, then cleaned the cabin.

He sprinkled seasonings on the steaks. He'd surprise

her and have dinner ready when she returned. Except, how long would she be?

Jamey held off on meal preparation and wandered the outer perimeter of the cabin, Bugsy traipsing beside him.

As they traversed the landscape, the gurgle of rushing water reached his ears. Following the sound, he and Bugsy discovered a river bordered by trees heavy with leaves.

Birds trilled overhead and a small wooden bridge allowed them to cross to the other side, where the landscape ascended in a field of evergreen and ponderosa pine trees.

The property was the perfect vacation hideaway. "Someday, Bugsy, we have to buy a place like this."

Bugsy trailed along, tail lifted high, nose twitching.

Why wouldn't Noreen want to spend every waking moment here?

They returned to the path and followed it to the cabin. How close were they to the sinkholes? Could they hike to the place? That would make their approach nearly invisible to the authorities guarding the entrances.

Jamey got the map out of his truck and went inside the cabin. After spreading it out on the dining table to study, he sighed. The sinkholes were at least ten miles southwest of their location. Too far to hike.

Bugsy moved to the door and whined.

"I agree, it's stuffy in here." Jamey opened the door and allowed her out.

He inhaled the fresh mountain air and trailed behind her. The cabin's spacious and breathtaking surroundings were truly mesmerizing. From the place where he stood, he spotted the rise and fall of the Black Hills. The setting was picturesque against the sky.

"Lord, I believe You've orchestrated this search. I'm limited in my human abilities. But You're unlimited. Guide us and grant us the wisdom to find Zia. Let Your will be done. Please bring Shaylee back safely."

Jamey exhaled and closed his eyes, and a mosquito buzzed by his ear, dragging him from the solace. He swatted it away and scanned the area.

Hidden beneath low-hanging tree branches was a gardening shed at the far side of the property.

"What do you suppose is in there?" Jamey asked Bugsy. She ignored him and approached the structure, nose in full force.

A chill in the air warned of a cool evening. He glanced at the cabin, remembering the woodburning stove inside. Firewood might be a good idea. He neared the shed, gaining a better view, and found a stack of logs perched against the side.

Jamey gathered several logs and carried them inside, then pulled out the dinner fixings and prepared the meal. He again glanced at the clock, concern weaving through him. If she wasn't back in the next twenty minutes, he'd go looking for her.

Daylight had nearly faded, forcing Jamey to turn on the lamps.

Shaylee should've already returned. How long could their meeting take?

He lifted his phone and started to call, then set it down. She'd asked him not to intrude on the meeting. If Noreen was providing important information, Shaylee needed her attention focused there. Plus, he didn't want to be that guy, demanding where she was and when she'd return.

But as the last shards of daylight threatened to disappear, his worry trumped, and he called Shaylee. The line rang once before transferring to voice mail.

Jamey snatched his keys just as his phone chimed with a text from Shaylee. Phone's almost dead. On my way.

He exhaled relief and stepped outside to watch for her return. He started the grill, went in and grabbed the steaks, situating them on the heated racks.

Where had Bugsy gone?

Jamey wandered the yard and spotted Bugsy scurrying to the gardening shed. He caught up with her. "What did you find?" He pushed aside the trees, exposing the padlocked door.

Bugsy's relentless interest in the shed increased Jamey's curiosity. Knocking down the dilapidated building door would be easy, but he'd respect the property.

He checked on the steaks and then went inside, locating a key on a ring hanging by the door. He returned to the shed as Bugsy continued her own search, moving around the perimeter.

He unlocked the door and pushed it wide. Using his phone's flashlight app, he illuminated the organized space filled with gardening tools and an old lawnmower. Bugsy moved around the space, sniffing intently, and lingered in the back corner. She sneezed as Jamey approached.

His foot bumped a shovel propped beside an old bag of cat food. Skittering across the floor caught his eye. He glanced down and spotted the twitching antennae of intruders disappearing into the shadows.

Cockroaches.

The rumble of an engine approached, and he quickly exited the shed. Shaylee's car zoomed down the road and skidded to a stop beside his truck. She jumped out. "Jamey!"

He rushed to her. Concern swarmed him. "What happened?"

"A bomb nearly killed us!" She gestured toward the grill. "Is something on fire?"

He spun and rushed to save the steaks. Shaylee joined him. Disbelief and guilt for not accompanying her consumed Jamey as she told him about the meeting with Noreen. "I never should have let you go alone! Why didn't you call me?"

Shaylee shook her head. "I think Noreen's phone, or possibly mine, was bugged and traced. How else could the killer know about the meeting? If they'd traced mine, they would've found us here. That hasn't happened. Noreen's in danger, too. When I told Captain Dugan, he agreed and traded me for a burner. He ordered me out of the area immediately."

"But you sent me a text."

She shook her head. "Dugan must have sent it—he's monitoring my phone. I told Noreen to get a burner and text me the number. Dugan handled the report, and I hurried back here."

Jamey pulled Shaylee into his arms. "That's it. You and I are not separating for one more second until we find this killer. It's not safe."

The burner phone rang, and Shaylee answered, putting it on speaker.

"Adler, are you okay?" Captain Dugan asked.

"Yes sir, I returned to the—"

"Don't say it!"

"Right. I'm with Jamey."

"Good. The fire investigator found an incendiary device. A trip wire set off the explosion."

"If Echo hadn't chased those geese, we would've been killed." She lifted the puppy and kissed her head.

"By the way, you got a text from an unknown number. I ran it, and it's a burner."

Shaylee quickly entered the number in the burner contacts. "Thank you. Jamey and I want to…" she hesitated "…to search tomorrow."

"On that note, I got word that backfill teams are moving up the schedule to work on the sinkholes."

"What? Why?" Shaylee asked.

"Baxter wants to cover up the bad press over the coffin situation with the positive about filling the holes and reopening the park."

Shaylee groaned. "How very kind of him. Ugh. Like when?"

"ASAP. I don't have to tell you if he gets his way, the evidence will be buried for good. It also means there will be more personnel working the area. If you're caught, there won't be much I can do to help you. He's got big names in his pocket. Wants it done before the swearing-in ceremony. Please, both of you, be careful. The killer is escalating."

"Proof we're getting closer. Baxter's trying to hide something."

"Exactly. His attacks will be more unpredictable and desperate. Keep me updated."

"Roger that," Shaylee acknowledged and disconnected. She tilted her head. "Why are you looking at me that way?"

"Most people would be angry God didn't protect them from the bomb in the first place, but instead, you're grateful because Echo chased the geese," Jamey said.

"It's easy to be grateful for the obvious things. It's all about perspective."

Jamey's heart warmed. Shaylee was an amazing lady.

"So, how soon can we head to the sinkholes?"

"Shaylee, you won't want to hear this, but are you absolutely certain you can trust Dugan? He's the only one with knowledge about what's going on. What if he's setting us up?"

"Jamey, Dugan is like family to me. After losing my parents and Zia, I had no one. Dugan and Franny embraced me. I trust him with my life."

He hoped she was right, because if not, Dugan would have the perfect setup for getting rid of them.

THIRTEEN

"Thank you for coming out this early." Shaylee passed the borrowed rope ladder to Jamey.

Captain Dugan nodded. "Technically, I was never here, remember?"

She grinned. "Right."

"I'd feel better going with you, but I'm old and will just end up being a liability." Dugan waggled his eyebrows.

"Hardly."

"You could always ask Noreen," Jamey grumbled.

Shaylee swatted playfully at him. "Stop that. She's harmless."

Dugan frowned disapproval. "Did you tell Noreen you're returning to the sinkholes today?"

"No, sir, only you."

"Good." Dugan stepped back. "I'll do what I can to delay the backfill teams until you've returned. Get on your way. Sunrise in less than an hour. As soon as you can, I want intel."

Jamey shook Dugan's hand. "Will do."

"Thanks." Shaylee lifted Echo from the truck. She passed the puppy to her boss. "Take good care of her."

Dugan took the dog with a smile and cradled her. "She's in good hands." He gave her a quick nod and slid into his truck.

She and Jamey climbed into his pickup and he reversed from the spot, then merged onto the road.

"What if something happens to Dugan? He's the only one who knows what we're doing. I hate to even think that way but after all we've been through—"

"I understand." Jamey's words were agreeable, but his tone had her wondering if he was still suspicious of her captain. "Involving anyone else is unwise."

"You're right." Shaylee sighed. Jamey's question about Dugan's trustworthiness niggled at her. She shoved it away. *You can't suspect everyone in your life.*

Shards of coral hues were developing on the horizon as Jamey parked behind towering rock formations.

They climbed out of the pickup, and Shaylee checked the contents of her backpack for the tenth time. Beef jerky, trail mix, granola bars and crackers should sustain them for the hike. The side pockets held bagged dog food and treats, as well as portable bowls. She added several water bottles from the cooler.

"I'll probably overheat with all these layers on," she commented.

"You'll be glad for them later," Jamey said.

"You think of everything." She watched as he secured the rope ladder on his pack along with the flashlights, GPS, flags and first aid kit.

"I thought it might be easier to descend and ascend into the sinkhole this way."

"That takes all the adventure out of this trip. I kind of enjoyed dropping straight through the earth in a death-defying feat."

Jamey laughed. "Maybe next time."

Shaylee slid into her backpack straps, tightening and securing them. It was heavy, but Jamey carried the greater weight in supplies, so she wouldn't complain.

Jamey slipped on Bugsy's harness and secured her leash.

As their final preparation, they covered the vehicle with a camouflage tarp, blending it with the thick tree cover.

They started out hiking past a lake that mirrored the sky in perfect replication. Gray, craggy cliffs surrounded the water, while sparse greenery dotted the landscape.

"I've lived in South Dakota my entire life, and I've never seen the places I have with you." Shaylee stood on a boulder, soaking up the mesmeric scenery.

"When it's always available, we take it for granted. You think you'll get around to visiting, but daily junk gets in the way."

"Definitely. When this is all over, I want to spend months hiking and camping out here."

"Wait, I thought you were a—what did you call it?—day trip kind of girl," Jamey quipped.

Shaylee laughed. "It's a woman's prerogative to change her mind."

"No argument here." Jamey lifted the portable GPS device. "This way."

They changed direction, moving away from the lake and ascending the path on the mountain. Shaylee enjoyed the cool breeze against her cheeks while Jamey and Bugsy took the lead.

Leaves rustled the trees, and the birds chorused in varying songs. Pine mingled with wood and dew beneath the canopy of foliage. Two squirrels chattered, chasing one another, but Bugsy appeared unmoved by the banter.

"Should be over this ridge," Jamey announced.

They ascended the mountain and Shaylee gasped, wanting to reach out and touch the rising orange orb set against the breathtaking colors of morning.

"God's an incredible artist," Jamey said.

Awe and wonder delayed her reply, and her heart warmed with love. "Yes, He is," she whispered.

"We need to get down this ridge to that valley. The sink-hole should be just past those rock formations."

Their boots crunched on the sandy trail. Sparse pine trees poked through the rocky ground in defiance of the rough soil.

"Overcomers," Shaylee said.

"What?" Jamey paused and turned to face her, standing tall against the picture-postcard background. She sucked in a breath. His cerulean eyes pierced her, and the rugged cut of his jaw and his masculine form sent her heart into an arrhythmia. "Are you okay?" He moved toward her, concern creasing his forehead.

Shaylee blinked, shoving down her thoughts. "I, uh, was just thinking how unlikely it is for those trees to grow here. The ground is so hard and yet they've forced through, making a way where there is none." She gestured to where a pine stood rooted in the narrow place between rock and earth. "They're overcomers."

"Like us," Jamey said.

They continued the steep descent down the ridge and into the valley. Conversation quieted and the reassurance God would be with them gave Shaylee peace.

"There, see it?" Jamey called, getting her attention. He lifted the binoculars, and she peered through, spotting the place they'd fallen through the first time.

A fresh infusion of energy coursed through her.

Jamey placed a hand on her shoulder "Go slow, listen for anything that sounds like the earth is giving way. Step carefully."

"Got it."

He reined in Bugsy. "Stay close."

They cautiously closed the distance to their destination.

As they neared the sinkhole, Shaylee exhaled, not realizing she'd held her breath the entire time.

She joined Jamey, kneeling beside the area. He tugged back debris that had partially covered the space, revealing the gaping hole.

"Has it grown wider?"

"Looks like it." Jamey lowered the rope ladder, securing the anchors above ground. He strapped Bugsy to his chest, using a different halter. "They're similar to the military's equipment," he explained.

"Very cool. Does it come in pink, though?"

He chuckled. "We'll have to check."

Shaylee went first and moved to the side, allowing Jamey room to descend.

Once their feet reached the ground, Jamey unstrapped Bugsy, permitting her to move freely, then passed Shaylee a flashlight. "Bugsy."

The dog sat, ears lifted in anticipation.

He stroked her short mane. "Ready to work?"

Bugsy's tail swished.

"Find Adam."

She sniffed the air, whiskers twitching.

"Find Adam," Jamey repeated.

Bugsy turned and headed through the tunnels.

Jamey and Shaylee followed close behind. The passageways were too narrow for them to walk side by side until they reached a Y in the cave.

"I don't remember going this way before," Shaylee said.

Jamey glanced around. "I don't, either."

Bugsy paused before entering a room to the right where white stone walls surrounded them. Debris covered the ground, which sloped and rose in erratic variations.

Shaylee scanned the area with her flashlight, searching for any evidence of Zia. Bugsy disappeared behind a staggering pile of rocks. "Is that the result of an avalanche?" Shaylee asked.

"Most likely."

Jamey and Shaylee followed and halted.

Bugsy sat beside a dirt mound. Using the beam, Shaylee illuminated the surroundings and spotted the shimmer.

She hurried and dropped to her knees, fingers digging through the soil. "It's Zia's wedding ring."

"Hold on." Jamey took pictures with his cell phone.

The exquisite piece of jewelry lay amid the debris, unattached, the massive diamond reflecting off Shaylee's flashlight beam.

Shaylee brushed away the earth, fully exposing the ring, and tucked it into her backpack. "There's got to be more here."

They worked to clear the dirt, and her hand grazed something hard.

The off-white appearance of a mandible stopped Jamey midswipe.

She gasped and fell back on her behind, her dirt-covered hand pressed against her mouth.

Jamey took pictures while emotions rolled over her in tidal waves.

The months of searching. The seed of hope that they'd find Zia alive somewhere was crushed by the reality of the remains partially exposed before her.

Unrestrained grief tore through Shaylee in a wail foreign to her own ears.

She doubled over, holding her stomach.

Jamey was at her side in an instant, pulling her tightly against his chest. She allowed him to absorb her brokenness, shielding her as she wept over the devastation of her loss.

Bugsy moved to their side, sitting quietly, as though she understood the magnitude of the moment.

When Shaylee had cried herself dry, she pushed back and Jamey released his hold but remained close, pressing a napkin into her hand.

Shaylee blew her nose. "I expected this moment. I never thought it would hit me with such force."

"I'm so sorry."

"Thank you for letting me fall apart."

"I'm grateful you allowed me to be here for you." Jamey sat beside her.

"The search is over. I'm taking Zia home." She choked on the last word and Jamey put an arm around her shoulder, hugging her.

"Let's get above ground and notify Dugan."

Shaylee nodded and pushed to her feet. "Without you and Bugsy, we never would've found Zia. I can't thank you enough. Now she'll rest in peace. And my heart can grieve her loss and move on. I couldn't before. I was stuck in limbo and there was no relief."

"I was just a party to what God intended to do." Jamey smiled. "I'll feel better once we get her out of here." His quiet strength was like a balm to the wounds of her heart. "Zia was blessed to have a sister so brave and dedicated."

Shaylee swiped away a stray tear and Jamey again reached for her. She leaned into his embrace and released her broken heart into his capable hands.

They had to keep moving. If Baxter had his way, the backfill teams would bury him and Shaylee forever. Loath to separate from her, he whispered, "We better get going."

"Yes."

Jamey used his GPS and phone to document with pictures the location for the rescue and recovery teams. He scanned the ceiling, catching a gap above. "It's almost like this avalanched through the ground."

"Then there might be more evidence around here." Shaylee moved past him, using her flashlight.

They worked on opposite sides, inspecting the surrounding area inside the compact room.

"Here!" she exclaimed, and Jamey rushed to where Shaylee knelt. "Get a picture before I dig it out." She exposed a hot pink strap and a circular bag. "Zia's purse. I always hated this one." She pulled it free and brushed off the dirt.

Jamey waited patiently as she inspected the contents.

"What's this?" She unfolded a photo and held it up.

Jamey illuminated the picture with his flashlight. "Noreen and Baxter."

Baxter had looped his arm around Noreen's shoulders. The couple's image portrayed polar opposite ways of dressing, although Noreen rivaled Baxter's six-foot-two-inch athletic build and stature. She wore a simple black gown, wrinkled and ill fitting, and her choice of sensible shoes didn't match the outfit. By contrast, Baxter sported a spotless, wrinkle-free tailored black suit, white shirt and matching tie.

"This was taken shortly before Zia disappeared. Some big hoopla event for Baxter. Hmm. That's really pretty." She pointed to an indoor waterfall sculpture in the background. "I don't remember it."

But Jamey's attention wasn't on the waterfall. "Check out Noreen."

"What?" Shaylee asked.

"Look at the way she's focused on Baxter." Noreen stood gazing at Baxter, her lips slightly parted in a wistful smile.

A frown creased Shaylee's forehead. "Enamored."

"Yes."

She shrugged. "Noreen is young and in awe of the guy."

"Are you sure? Were they having an affair?"

Shaylee snorted. "Um. No. Noreen isn't like that and Baxter wouldn't look twice at her. He wanted someone beautiful and refined like Zia."

Jamey remained unconvinced. "For the sake of argument, could Zia have stumbled on something going on between them?"

"Okay, for the sake of argument, I suppose that's possible. But doubtful."

"People have killed for less than a discovered infidelity. In Baxter's case, if Zia went to the press with his indiscretions, it would ruin his campaign. That's motive."

"But that doesn't explain the accounting journal? Did Zia uncover Baxter's money laundering or something like that?"

"I'd say we have a couple of strong motives," Jamey agreed.

"Baxter is going down."

Jamey set up flags around the site. "Once they exhume Zia's remains, and we have forensic evidence, the rest will fall into place. Are you ready to go?"

Shaylee pocketed the picture, then paused, taking one last look. "Yes."

The trek to the entrance was somber. They neared the sinkhole, and Shaylee touched his arm. "You've been super quiet."

"Lost in thought."

Voices carried through the hollow space, growing in volume and intensity. Shaylee glanced at him, her eyebrows peaking.

They approached with caution, listening and keeping Bugsy reined in. As they neared the Y in the passageway, they stayed out of sight. Jamey mouthed, "Off," shutting down his flashlight and plunging them into darkness. He gripped Bugsy's halter handle.

"You can't do this," a female voice pleaded.

Shaylee moved closer and whispered, "That's Noreen!"

"You should've stayed away. I told you!" a male voice raged.

"No. Please! Don't do this."

A gunshot and a scream.

Jamey flipped on his flashlight, and they charged through the passageway to the opening.

Noreen Liddle lay beneath the sinkhole entrance.

Shaylee pressed fingers against Noreen's neck. "She's still alive but bleeding profusely. It's a good thing I dressed in layers." She removed her button-down shirt, revealing the blue T-shirt underneath, and held it against Noreen's chest wound.

Jamey spotted a knife near the ladder and followed the braids to where the severed line left one side swinging above precariously.

He knelt, using his sleeve to lift the knife where a jagged section of the handle was missing.

Movement above.

A shift.

Jamey looked up just as a thud landed beside him.

A grenade!

Jamey hoisted Noreen onto his shoulders. "Run!"

They bolted into the depths of the cave and didn't stop running until the blast echoed behind them.

Jamey glanced over his shoulder, spotting the cloud of dust and debris filling the space like an ominous smoke screen. "Keep going!"

They rounded a corner just as a slam shook their surroundings. Jamey turned, using the flashlight to peer back.

The ceiling had collapsed. Rock, old wooden beams and dirt blocked the passageway. They wouldn't return the way they'd come.

"We're trapped."

Wide-eyed, Shaylee swallowed hard.

Jamey lifted Noreen. "There has to be another way out of here." *Lord, please let it be so.*

The convoluted maze made up of larger and smaller rooms and passageways that dead-ended had them taking three steps forward and two steps back. Jamey's mind raced. Dugan had given them the ladder. Had he loosened the braids, then cut it? Who else would've known to do so? And Dugan was the only one aware of their location. The male voice was familiar but muffled. But surely Shaylee would've recognized Dugan's voice and said so? Questions bombarded him from every direction.

Finally, they came to a hollowed-out room in the mine and he set down Noreen.

"We have to get her help," Shaylee said.

Jamey reached into his pocket and withdrew the knife, passing it to her. "Shaylee, check this out."

"There's a piece missing."

"Yeah, and that looks an awful lot like the one Bugsy found at your house."

Shaylee's gaze dropped to Noreen. "No. It's not possible." She knelt beside her. "Noreen, can you hear me?"

The unconscious woman didn't move.

"Once we get out of here, we'll have the answer."

Shaylee frowned and nodded. "How did she know how to find us?"

"That is a brilliant question." Jamey hesitated, then voiced his concern. "Shaylee, Dugan gave us the rope ladder."

She locked eyes with him. "Don't go there. Dugan would never do anything to hurt us. Besides, why give us the ladder, then cut the ropes?"

"Baxter's reach is long. Could Dugan be working with Noreen?"

Shaylee rubbed her neck. "No. And speculating won't help right now."

Was she right? *Lord, we need wisdom. We aren't sure who our enemy is, but You are. Bring the truth to light.*

"What do we do now?" Shaylee's question jolted Jamey to the present.

"There's nothing we can do but keep going. We'll head that way." He pointed to an opening.

"Okay."

Jamey hoisted Noreen over his shoulder in a fireman's carry.

A bark echoed, bouncing off the stone walls.

He turned, but Bugsy was gone.

Jamey's stomach sank into his boots. Had the collapse buried her? "Bugsy!"

His words echoed back to him.

"Where did she go?" Shaylee swung the flashlight, searching the area. "Bugsy!"

Jamey shifted Noreen to gain a better hold. "We have to find her!"

"If she hears us calling, will it confuse her with the echoes?" Shaylee whispered.

Jamey refused to speak aloud his doubt. He prayed that Bugsy would respond and return to them.

She couldn't be…no, he wouldn't dare think the words.

They trailed through the labyrinth calling Bugsy's name, though the way the sound reverberated, he agreed, it might only confuse her.

Shaylee picked up speed, rushing toward a small pile of logs in varying shapes and lengths between two rotting wooden support beams. She stopped short when her foot hit the side, causing a shift to the logs. Worried they'd fall and hurt her, Jamey cried, "Don't move!"

She froze.

"Sorry. Let me take a look." He lowered Noreen, then moved to inspect the space.

The opening was too small for them to crawl through. A sharp bark came from the other side.

"Bugsy's there!" Shaylee said.

Jamey surveyed the area. "We can't get through it, and moving the logs will create an avalanche that could bring the ceiling down, too."

But Bugsy was behind that wall. Trapped, and Jamey wouldn't leave her behind.

Jamey knelt, peering through the space. "Bugsy!"

FOURTEEN

Shaylee knelt beside Noreen, concern mingling with confusion for her friend. They needed to keep moving and find a way out of the mine, but not without Bugsy. The barking had come and gone, as though the dog ran from one end to the other before eventually fading altogether. Jamey had gone hoarse calling Bugsy's name, and the lack of the response had left him distressed.

She checked Noreen's wound and gasped at the increased bleeding. If they didn't get Noreen help soon, she would die. "She was fighting with Baxter."

Jamey faced her. Was that relief on his face? "Are you certain?"

Shaylee bit her lip. "Honestly? Not one hundred percent. The man's voice was muffled, so it's difficult to say for sure. I'm certain I recognize the voice, though."

"Did it sound like Dugan?"

Irritation swelled. "Dugan is not a criminal."

"I'm sorry, Shaylee. I'm just trying to reason through the possibilities."

"Well, get that one out of your mind."

Jamey nodded. "Is it possible she was fighting with the intruder who broke into your house?"

Shaylee pondered his question while trying to recall the voice. "No. I mean…maybe? But I really think it sounded like Baxter." Or did she want to pin it on Baxter so badly she was forcing the evidence? "Noreen will tell us when she comes to." She brushed aside the sweaty strands of hair from her friend's forehead.

Shaylee turned to the avalanche of logs and peered through the opening. How long had Bugsy been missing? The grenade and explosion had decimated the section of the cave where they'd begun. They hadn't heard any more barking.

She swallowed hard. Jamey hadn't mentioned it, but surely he wondered the same thing. Had the collapse buried Bugsy? No. She wouldn't allow her imagination to process the possibility. It was too horrid to consider.

A loud groan reverberated through the cavernous walls.

Shaylee jumped to her feet.

Jamey put out an arm, keeping her close to the stone. She looked up, surveying the rough gypsum ceiling with its jagged edges rising and falling. Inching around the perimeter, they maneuvered around the corner and peered out to view the passageway.

Jamey shone his flashlight into the abyss where the light faded into black. An ominous second groan warned of impending danger.

Neither spoke.

Or dared to breathe.

Then an earth-shattering crash sent dust in an all-consuming cloud rushing toward them. Jamey grabbed her arm and tugged her back into the hollowed-out area. They squatted beside Noreen to shield her, then pulled the necklines of their shirts up over their noses and mouths.

Shaylee's legs shook with exertion as they waited for the dust and debris to settle again.

When at last they uncovered their faces, Shaylee looked at the place where they assumed Bugsy had entered.

"Jamey!"

He turned.

Debris blocked the opening.

Jamey rushed to the logs, tugging on them. "Bugsy! Bugsy!" His desperate cries gripped Shaylee's heart.

Her eyes welled with tears.

"Help me! We have to clear this." The immense debris had avalanched over the space.

Shaylee went to him and touched his shoulder. "Jamey. It's no use. We can't move that and if we do, we might cause a worse collapse."

"She's in there, though! How will Bugsy get out?"

"The barking faded. She might've found another way out. There is. She'll find it. We'll move through and call her. This place is a maze. We'll find her." Shaylee spoke quickly, assuring herself as much as Jamey.

Devastation hung on his shoulders and he stood, shoulders hunched in defeat. "Okay."

He lifted Noreen again in a firefighter's carry, and they exited the space, walking to the closest of the remaining passageways.

"Bugsy!" Shaylee and Jamey took turns crying out.

At every opening, break in the wall, or space, they stopped and peered, searching.

With each failed attempt, her hope dwindled.

A muffled sound caught her attention. Jamey must've heard it, too, because he hesitated. "Did you hear that?"

"Yes."

Neither dared to breathe.

Again the sharp noise.

Muffled, but increasing in volume.

Barking! But the echo made it hard to determine which direction the sound came from.

"Bugsy!" Jamey cried.

Her canine greeting responded louder this time.

Shaylee and Jamey rushed through a smaller cavern

and climbed over a barrier, halting at a towering set of gypsum rocks.

Bugsy appeared in the space between a stone wall and rushed at Jamey and Shaylee, soaking wet, tail wagging.

Jamey dropped to his knees, careful not to drop Noreen, who remained unconscious. He set her down and pulled Bugsy into his arms, laughing as she lavished him with kisses.

Shaylee watched, enjoying the outpouring of affection from Bugsy's soggy form.

"How did you get wet?" Jamey's relief oozed through his voice as he loved on Bugsy.

"She found water!"

Jamey stood and walked to the opening. He turned and faced Shaylee. "It's big enough for us to pass through, but it'll be tight carrying Noreen."

"I'll go first and check it out."

Jamey leashed Bugsy. "Sorry, girl, but we're not going through that turmoil again."

Proceeding, Shaylee maneuvered between the stone walls. "It's tight but doable."

Jamey squeezed through behind her.

The rocks separated into wider spaces and opened into an expansive cavern where a small stream flowed.

"Wow."

"Gypsum Cave 101 says the water source will lead outside."

"Great job, Bugsy! Show us the way out of here," Shaylee said.

The dog scurried ahead, keeping to the edge of the stream. The brownish water was only a couple of inches deep.

"This is amazing," Shaylee breathed, her flashlight bouncing off the walls where tool marks remained.

Their lights blended with sunlight, piercing the darkness through a circular opening.

"Yes!" Shaylee screeched with joy.

Relief mingled on Jamey's face with the droplets of perspiration, no doubt from the effort of carrying Noreen. "We'll have to work together," he said.

Shaylee crawled through and worked with Jamey to hoist Noreen up and out of the cave. They did the same with Bugsy and he emerged last.

Sitting outside, they soaked up the warmth of the sun while Jamey updated the GPS.

Shaylee checked the burner. "No reception."

"Send a text to Dugan, requesting an ambulance. If nothing else, it might go through as soon as the device connects," Jamey suggested.

"Good idea." She sent the message and he resecured Bugsy's leash.

"I'm eating the biggest chocolate cake I can find when this is done. I'll have earned my workout."

"Sign me up for that. In fact, I'm buying." Shaylee grinned. "Are we that far from the truck?"

"You really don't want the answer to that question." Jamey grunted, hefting Noreen onto his shoulders.

They traipsed along the brush where the rocky land rose in the distance, having emerged at the foot of the mountain range. They'd have to climb to the hiking path. Shaylee almost hoped the authorities spotted them so they'd get to help faster. It would be worth it for Noreen's sake.

Neither spoke as they made their way through the wilderness. Both anxious and tired from the trek.

Shaylee wanted to offer to carry Noreen, but knowing it wasn't a possibility, she refrained. As they crested the hill near the lake, hope infused Shaylee. They were almost to the truck.

Even Bugsy seemed to be eager to get out of the mountains. When they finally reached the place where they'd left Jamey's truck, their relief turned to confusion.

No truck.

Shaylee looked around. "Did we go the wrong way?"

"No." Jamey set down Noreen and swiped a hand over his head. "This is unbelievable. He stole my truck." He pointed to the tire tracks in the dirt.

"How did they find us?"

Jamey didn't answer her, and she didn't press.

Shaylee lifted the burner and Jamey did the same with his phone, both searching for reception and coming up void.

"I guess we head for the main road. Surely a worker or guard will see us."

Jamey grunted. "I've never wanted to be caught by the police more in my life."

The path required hiking a steep embankment separated by a deep ravine. Carrying Noreen couldn't have been an easy feat, but Jamey never complained.

When they finally crested the embankment and traipsed through the tree line bordering the road, they rested next to a boulder.

Jamey settled Noreen beside them. "We have to get her help soon."

"Someone will drive by. I hope." Shaylee removed bottles of water, passed one to Jamey and filled a bowl for Bugsy.

As the temperature rose, the shelter of the trees helped shade them, but Noreen's face and hairline were damp with perspiration.

The soft hum of an approaching car infused optimism in Shaylee. She hurried toward the center of the road, lifting Jamey's binoculars. "Someone's coming!"

She waited until the car got closer, then stepped forward, waving her arms wildly. "Here! Stop!"

The dark sedan with tinted windows cruised at a steady pace in the oncoming lane. He flashed his lights to indicate he'd spotted Shaylee, and she scurried to the side. The driver did the same, slowing as he drew near, but she was unable to see him through the illegally tinted glass.

Shaylee glanced over her shoulder and gathered the leash from Jamey. "He's stopping."

Jamey hoisted Noreen and rushed to her side. "Finally."

They approached, and the car stopped.

A second ticked by and Shaylee's instincts blared on high alert.

Without warning, the car accelerated, tires screeching as he sped right for them.

Shaylee jerked Bugsy to the side, but the driver swerved, determined to hit them. A gun emerged from the driver's partially lowered window.

"Get down!" Shaylee screamed.

Jamey and Shaylee ducked the rapid gunfire.

The car grazed the edge of the shoulder, forcing them off the road.

The sandy ground caused them to slip, landing on their behinds as they tumbled off the shoulder and slid down the embankment. Shaylee lost hold of the leash.

Branches and rocks zipped past. The force of descent was so fast she struggled to grasp something to stop her fall. Something ripped at her shirt, but she didn't see what.

The car's engine roared, fading into the distance.

"Lord, help us!"

Jamey clung to Noreen, legs stretched out in front of him to ward off the branches and rocks. At last, his boot hooked on a boulder and they halted. His chest heaved, and he searched the area for Shaylee.

Bugsy sat above him, whining and pacing, unable to make the sharp descent.

Shaylee lay sprawled to his left, hands clutching a flowering bush. She turned her head and faced him. "Are you all right?"

The woman was amazing. She clung for life and yet worried for him. "Yeah. You?"

"I think so."

"Bugsy, stay," Jamey ordered.

She dropped to a sit, body trembling to obey, yet her soulful eyes pierced him with silent pleas to run to his side.

"Hold on and I'll crawl to you." Shaylee scrambled to her knees and made her way to him along the steep incline. "I'll hold on to Noreen while you regain your balance."

She inched across the rocky terrain, reaching for him. Shaylee sat and hooked Noreen's arms around her knees while Jamey got to his feet. Establishing a stronger standing position, he hoisted Noreen onto his shoulders and together they hiked up the embankment.

The assailant had disappeared, leaving the road desolate once more. Jamey moved to a large boulder beneath a sheltering of pine trees and settled Noreen on the ground.

"I don't think he'll return, but we're hidden here," Jamey said.

"At least he didn't stop to see if we were dead."

"Exactly."

Shaylee removed her phone. "I have reception!" She quickly called Dugan, providing him an update on the situation.

Jamey attended to Bugsy, ensuring she was free from injury, then unfolded her portable bowl and filled it with water.

"Yes, sir. Near the first tunnel. Thank you." Shaylee disconnected. "Your plan worked. Dugan got the message before I called. He's got a BOLO out for the car and your truck, and he agreed Baxter's coming in for questioning."

"The killer might outrun us, but he'll never escape the radio or a Be on the Lookout message," Jamey said.

"He won't get far."

Jamey passed Shaylee a bottle of water and they sat on the boulder.

"Dugan's already got rescue headed this way, so it shouldn't be long."

"That's the best news I've heard all day." Jamey checked on Noreen again. Her eyes fluttered. He knelt and the object he'd found at Shaylee's apartment and placed in his pocket now poked his leg. Removing the item from the bag, he held it up. "We need to get this to the evidence technician."

Shaylee's eyes widened, and she placed a hand to her throat. "We have to return to the cabin."

"Why?" Jamey searched her, waiting for an explanation.

She shook her head and looked down. "Because I know where that piece came from. I'll notify Dugan we need to stop at the cabin on our way to pick up Baxter." She withdrew her phone and typed in a message. After a few moments, it buzzed and she said, "Dugan wants a deputy to accompany us to the cabin and handle Baxter."

The blare of sirens screamed across the mountain range, and from their vantage point, Jamey spotted the swirling red and blue lights approaching.

As the emergency vehicles drew closer, Shaylee stepped out from the shelter and waved them down. An ambulance followed by two patrol cars pulled to the shoulder.

Two paramedics jumped out, and within minutes they had loaded Noreen onto a stretcher. One called vitals into his radio and climbed into the back of the ambulance while the driver slid behind the wheel. "We're headed to Black Hills Memorial."

"Please request security over her. No visitors, and a

guard posted outside her door. She's a suspect," Shaylee said.

"Got it."

The ambulance sped away. The officers parked behind the rig were deep in discussion.

"I know that deputy," Shaylee said. "I'll be right back."

Jamey nodded, grateful he didn't have to go with her. They glanced in his direction periodically, making him uncomfortable. He reined in Bugsy while Shaylee spoke to the taller of the two men. He locked eyes with Jamey. Great.

Shaylee returned. "Dugan already updated them on our situation. Well, within reason, anyway. I texted him we're on our way to the cabin. Deputy Tips will drive us."

They reached the first patrol car, but the deputies were engaged in conversation at the second vehicle.

"I'll tell them we're ready," Shaylee said.

Jamey and Bugsy slid in the back seat. She seemed unaware that the steel cage sent a wedge of fear and intimidation through him.

Shaylee and Deputy Tips returned and climbed into the front seat. He listened as she updated Tips on the situation and didn't miss the way her leveled tone revealed professionalism rather than emotion. Grateful they didn't engage him in the discussion, he closed his eyes, warding off the exhaustion from the day.

"This is it." Shaylee's voice drew Jamey to the present, and he glanced out the window.

They'd arrived at the cabin.

Jamey waited for Shaylee to open the back passenger door, freeing him and Bugsy.

The deputy turned to face him, wagging a finger as a smile emerged. "I thought I recognized you."

Jamey's stomach tightened. *Lord, give me wisdom.*

"You're that supersmart Bug Dude."

Would he ever shed that wretched nickname? Jamey busied himself with Bugsy's leash. "That's me."

"Deputy Tips. Pleasure to meet you, sir." He offered a hand.

Jamey looked up and blinked several times, uncertain he'd heard him correctly. Shaylee nudged him in the side, jolting him. Finally, he shook the man's hand. "Jamey Dyer, and Bugsy, respectfully."

"I've seen you testify a few times. Truly amazing, man. You make bugs seem cool. My thirteen-year-old son wants to be an entomologist, too."

He'd misjudged Tips's intentions. "Thank you, Deputy. If your kid ever wants to talk insects, let me know."

"Really? Oh, he'd love that!" Tips grinned.

Jamey smiled, genuinely. "Anytime."

"Cool. All right. How can I help here?"

"Would you mind keeping an eye out here for any danger while we run inside?" Shaylee asked.

"No prob." Tips gave a nod.

The sight of the old cabin was refreshing, but Jamey placed a hand on Shaylee's arm, stilling her in the shadows. "Are you sure it's safe?"

Shaylee used his binoculars and scanned the area. "No, but I guess we'll find out soon enough."

Jamey inhaled. "Right. Well, let's do this."

Trepidation hovered as they neared the cabin. Cautiously they moved around the perimeter, checking for intruders, then walked to the door. Jamey pushed it wide and stepped inside. Everything was as they'd left it that morning.

Jamey hesitated.

"Something wrong?" Shaylee glanced around.

"Deputy Tips wasn't who I expected. Perception is reality," he mumbled.

"Oh, because it never occurred to you cops are impressed with your skills?" Shaylee asked.

"Guess I need to change my perspective."

Shaylee squeezed his shoulder and smiled sadly, no doubt reminded of all they still needed to do. "Let's finish this. Captain Dugan headed to the site, so the team should already have started exhuming Zia's remains." Her voice quivered on the last word. "Do you still have the knife?"

He removed the knife and the piece they'd found at Shaylee's house earlier, placing them on the table.

"I'll be right back." She moved to the main floor bedroom.

Jamey poured food into a bowl for Bugsy and Shaylee returned carrying a thin wooden box, which she set on the table and opened. "I knew it looked familiar." She lifted a matching knife and held it up for Jamey to see.

"It's a match! That proves Noreen cut the rope and maybe worked with Baxter to hire the thug who broke into your house."

Shaylee frowned. "Not necessarily. I don't believe she'd hurt me. And what about the bomb? She could've died, too. That doesn't make sense. What if she came to the sinkhole to warn us? Did Baxter set her up?"

"Anything is possible." But Jamey remained unconvinced that Noreen was innocent.

Bugsy whined at the door. They exited the cabin, and she immediately rushed to the gardening shed.

"Cockroaches!" He jogged to catch up.

"What?" Shaylee hurried to his side.

Jamey opened the door and stepped in. "I spotted cockroaches here when you returned last night. But in the craziness of saving our dinner and the bomb story, I spaced it."

Bugsy was already sniffing at the back of the shed.

The space was too tight for both of them to stand side

by side, so Shaylee remained behind him. "What did she find?"

"I don't know, but you'd better believe I'm paying attention."

Bugsy walked to the far corner and sat, indicating. Jamey lifted a tarp that appeared thrown haphazardly over the space. A complete contradiction to the organized status of the shed's contents. He revealed a shovel leaning against the wall and a pair of dirt-caked boots concealed underneath.

"What's there?" Shaylee asked.

"Let's get into the light and inspect these."

They stepped out of the shed and the afternoon sun provided them with a clearer view of the boots. Jamey spotted rust-colored marks across the brown leather.

"Is that blood?"

"I think so." He set them down and returned for the shovel, bringing it out to the light, as well. Smears of white speckled the bottom. "Gypsum."

Shaylee met his gaze. Triumph and sorrow mingled in her eyes.

He glanced down, inspecting the boots. An object inside caught his eye. "Um, Shaylee."

She moved beside him, and he carefully withdrew a small leather book.

"It's the accounting journal." Shaylee flipped through the pages. "Look at this! There's an entry from DeChace, and you can see where a page was ripped out."

"Who's that?"

"DeChace is a known criminal with heavy dealings in money laundering." She turned the open page for him to see.

Jamey spotted the excessively sizable sum listed. "Whoa."

"This proves Baxter was keeping two sets of books. We got him!"

"On the money issue, but not for murder." He inspected the boots. "Once they process them, we will have our answers."

Jamey rushed to the house and grabbed a small plastic container and lid. He returned to the shed and collected several of the cockroaches, placing them inside. He came out holding the bowl and Shaylee cringed. "Please keep those away from me."

He laughed. "Do you have katsaridaphobia?"

"Huh?"

"Fear of cockroaches," Jamey interpreted.

"No, all bugs, thank you very much."

"Oh, then you have entomophobia. So, you're not interested in learning about them?"

She winced and shuddered. "Not even a little bit."

"They might provide a connection, though. I keep thinking about the cockroach in the coffin. Wish I'd taken it when I had the chance."

"Bugs in the outdoors aren't uncommon."

"No, but cockroaches travel in groups. I think that particular one got into the casket before the transport. The slick walls prevented his escape. And Baxter doesn't seem like he'd tolerate an infestation."

Shaylee considered his words. "True."

"Noreen is looking really good for this."

She shook her head. "He could have framed her. This is all inconclusive. Circumstantial evidence."

"Your optimism astounds me."

"I'll admit, if Noreen knew Baxter murdered Zia, she might have considered it her obligation to help him cover it up. For the record, I still don't think that's what happened, but for the sake of argument, it's a possibility. Once she comes to, we'll confront her with the evidence. Maybe she'll turn on him."

"Let's get this to the crime scene investigator for processing."

They walked to Deputy Tips and Shaylee made the call before updating the officer. They waited for the woman's arrival and Shaylee said, "She was on her way to the site, so she'll stop here first."

"Can you trust this person?" Jamey asked.

"I trust God. He's with us in this. And I sent a text message with pictures to Dugan, too."

"Right." He nodded.

The crime scene investigator arrived and took possession of the items, impressing Jamey with her professionalism and the care with which she documented the evidence.

Shaylee called Dugan but got no answer. She left a detailed message, and with Deputy Tips leading them, Shaylee and Jamey loaded into her car and drove to Baxter's estate.

"What will Tips do?" Jamey asked, dreading her answer. "He can't arrest Baxter without confirmation of the evidence."

Shaylee gripped the steering wheel tighter. "Not yet, but Dugan agrees Baxter is a person of interest and wants him brought in for questioning. I want to see Baxter's face when I tell him we found Zia. I'm confronting him with the murder charge. He'll confess. He has to. And if he gets wind we escaped, he'll try to run. This time, he won't get away again."

FIFTEEN

Shaylee's irrational hope that Baxter would fall at her feet confessing his role in Zia's murder was stupid, but optimism was free. At the moment. Regardless, she couldn't risk the criminal escaping before she confronted him. And although Dugan wanted Tips to handle bringing in Baxter, Shaylee didn't want to miss a moment of the discussion.

She pulled up to the property, where a soft glow illuminated the lower-level windows. Deputy Tips parked his patrol car in front of the house and the group exited their vehicles.

"Doesn't appear Baxter is home," Tips said.

Shaylee growled. "Of course he isn't."

Jamey moved along the perimeter and called, "You'll want to see this."

They joined him and peered through the window where he pointed. "Look familiar?"

Shaylee spotted the same indoor waterfall they'd seen in the picture. "I need a closer view." She tried the window. Locked.

"I'm pretty sure breaking and entering is still illegal," Jamey reminded.

"I'd have to agree," Tips said.

She frowned. "Right. I need a warrant to enter, but if

I give Baxter a heads-up, he'll get rid of it. Do you still have binoculars?"

Jamey rushed to the car and returned with them.

Shaylee looked through the window. "Look, there on the side. Is that an engraved letter *Z*?" She passed the binoculars to him.

"Possibly. I can't see it up close, but I'm more interested in the plexiglass. The same material the coffin was made of."

Shaylee pondered the implication. "Maybe Zia made the waterfall? There might be more evidence inside the house. I need a warrant."

"Did she do stuff like that?"

"Zia had many interests. Everything she touched came out beautifully. It's certainly possible." Shaylee averted her eyes, focused on a lawn ornament. "Truth is, after Baxter managed to prevent her from seeing me, we sort of lost touch before she—" She looked away. "I guess there was a lot about her life I missed."

Jamey placed a hand on her shoulder. "Don't do that to yourself." He lifted the binoculars again. "Let's focus on finishing this. Can you get a warrant to search the house?"

"I'm going to try."

"Let me know if I can help," Tips said.

"Thanks." Shaylee and Jamey shook his hand.

Her phone rang. "Dugan! I've got him." She blurted out the evidence from the shed and waterfall.

"Slow down. I'll detain Baxter, get here ASAP," Dugan said.

"He's there?"

"Yes, arrived a little while ago at the site. I had to get to a place where I'd have reception to call you."

"Arrest him, and I need a warrant for his house."

"One step at a time. I'm headed back to the site."

"I'm on my way!" They disconnected, and Shaylee addressed Tips. "We have to return to the site."

He jumped into his car, following as she drove as quickly as the speed limit permitted.

At the gate, Shaylee flashed her badge and the security moved aside allowing entry.

A variety of law enforcement emergency vehicles surrounded the area, making it easy to locate the site. Shaylee parked beside the other cop cars and stepped out. She rushed to where Baxter stood talking with Dugan, Echo at his feet.

"Detective Adler." Dugan's greeting was thick with warning.

Shaylee ignored it.

Jamey released Bugsy and she caught up to Echo.

Baxter faced them, tears streaming from his eyes. He rushed to Shaylee, arms outstretched. "Thank you for finding her! My sweet Zia."

Baxter pulled her into a bear hug. Stunned, she gaped at Jamey awkwardly, trying to decide whether to slug Baxter or offer him a Kleenex.

She decided on pushing him away, but Baxter released his hold and reached for Jamey's hand, pumping it wildly. "And you and your dog are to thank!"

Bugsy moved beside Jamey, sniffing at Baxter.

"I got word Noreen's at the hospital. I've contacted the best doctors in town to provide her care. She's such an asset. I cannot imagine who would do something so heinous. And it's all my fault. It's probably me they're trying to destroy, by going after the people I care most about," Baxter rambled.

Dugan nodded at Shaylee.

"About that. Baxter, we found evidence at the cabin. A knife used to cut the rope ladder before Noreen fell and we overheard her arguing with a man. With you."

Shaylee caught a glimpse of Dugan's disapproving frown. *Sorry, boss.*

Baxter's eyes widened and he plastered a hand against his expensive suit coat. "Me? No. I've never been here. What cabin? I don't have a clue what you're talking about."

"The cabin Noreen's grandmother owned," Jamey said.

Baxter tilted his head. "That's news to me."

"Oh, please," Shaylee snapped.

"Noreen is my employee. I keep everything very professional with her." He studied them. "Wait! You think—? No. Is it possible Noreen did this?" He gazed past her, where crews worked to excavate Zia's remains.

Shaylee swallowed. "Do you own a dark sedan with tinted windows?"

Baxter smiled. "No. I live in South Dakota. Four-wheel drive vehicles are a better investment."

"We were nearly run over on the road."

"Certainly you don't assume it was me? Did you see the driver?" Baxter argued.

Shaylee continued, ignoring him. "We also found an accounting journal in the boots, with the shovel used to bury Zia at the cabin. The same book the journal page I confronted you came from."

Baxter hung his head. "Fine. That I cannot refute. Yes, it's true. I took money from DeChace. It started out as a conversation, but he blackmailed me. What else could I do?"

"You used the same material to make the clear coffin you buried me in as well as the indoor waterfall at your house." Shaylee couldn't stop herself; the words tumbled out in rapid succession.

Baxter shook his head. "Coffin? Buried you? Shaylee, what are you talking about?"

"Don't play dumb!" She shook with adrenaline.

"Adler." Dugan's warning was low.

Baxter sighed. "Noreen made the waterfall for me. A gift."

The *Z* was an *N*. Realization flooded Shaylee. Had she blamed Baxter unjustly?

His hand flew to his mouth. "Oh no. She did it! Noreen killed Zia? I was aware she had unhealthy feelings for me, but I never dreamed she'd take it so far. I guess her obsession overruled her actions." Baxter's expression conveyed sadness. He stood taller, resuming his impeccable posture. "Still, I won't abandon her. Clearly, she needs help."

In her peripheral vision, Jamey bristled.

"It was you, Baxter," Shaylee insisted.

"Shaylee, we haven't had the best relationship, and I don't blame you for hating me if it makes you feel better. But I didn't kill Zia. And if Noreen did all of the horrible things you say, she must be held accountable. No loose ends. But she's still a kid—there'll be leniency for her."

Shaylee bit her lip. Was it true? Had Noreen committed all of the crimes?

"Taking money from DeChace is inexcusable. I justified my actions with the intentions of eliminating culprits like DeChace. It's for the greater good. But I'm no murderer. Just a stupid man whose financial means couldn't keep up with his political ambitions. For that I'm truly sorry." Baxter's speech was award-winning emotional, but instinct left Shaylee disbelieving.

Her attention reverted to Bugsy. She hadn't stopped sniffing Baxter. And now she sat beside him. "Is she indicating?" Shaylee asked Jamey, who appeared as intrigued with the scene.

Baxter ignored her and continued rambling his justifications.

Jamey moved around Baxter and shone a flashlight at the bottom of the man's expensive light gray suit pants. "Um, Shaylee."

Baxter hesitated as she circled behind him. Anger warmed her cheeks. "If you're innocent and you weren't here earlier, you might want to explain why there's blood on the back of your pants. And if we test your hands and clothes, we'll find gunshot residue."

Baxter jumped back. "What? Absolutely not!"

"Bugsy triggered on you because you have blood on your clothes," Jamey explained.

"No!" Baxter spun and reached into his suit coat, withdrawing a gun.

His arm snaked around Shaylee's neck, dragging her backward. He pressed the gun against her temple. "Move and I'll shoot."

"Take him out," Shaylee said, hands clutching his arm.

Bugsy barked and lunged at Baxter. Surprised, he stumbled sideways, tripping over Echo.

Shaylee and Baxter tumbled to the ground.

She rolled out from his hold, but he lay on his back, gun still trained on her. "You ruin everything! I should've killed you the first time, when I had the chance."

Several other officers drew their weapons.

"Drop the gun, Baxter. It's over," Dugan said.

Echo moved beside Shaylee, and Bugsy rushed to join them. She stood protectively in front of them, emitting a low growl.

Baxter blinked.

"She will attack," Shaylee warned, unsure if it was true. "Give me the gun."

Baxter dropped the weapon. "I had to stop Noreen. No loose ends. Don't you see? For the greater good? One life to save the lives of many."

"You're unbelievable." Shaylee wrenched his hands behind his back.

Dugan passed her a set of cuffs. "You've waited a long time for this."

"Baxter Heathcote, you're under arrest for Zia's murder, the attempted murder of Noreen Liddle, Jamey Dyer and myself. And any other charges I can stick to you." Shaylee secured the handcuffs and smiled at Jamey.

Jamey pushed open the door, allowing Shaylee to enter the hospital. Dugan trailed behind her and Jamey followed with the dogs.

She was on a mission and he wouldn't dare stand in her way.

A security guard stepped in their path. "Animals aren't allowed in here."

Jamey hesitated.

"Go on. I'll stay behind with them," Dugan said.

Did he trust the man? He couldn't leave Shaylee alone. "Thank you." Jamey reluctantly passed the leashes and followed Shaylee to where the unit nurse sat behind a desk shaped like a half-moon.

"Good evening. Detective Shaylee Adler. We're here to see Noreen Liddle."

The nurse checked the file. "Room 353."

Jamey glanced over his shoulder. Dugan was kneeling beside the dogs, lavishing them with affection. Bugsy's tail wagged. Jamey grinned. They'd be fine.

When he and Shaylee reached Noreen's room, they spotted a uniformed officer standing guard. Shaylee showed him her badge and he nodded and stepped aside. "Has she had any visitors?"

"No, ma'am, although Baxter Heathcote stopped by while she was in surgery."

"Thank you."

Jamey remained behind Shaylee as she took the lead. This was her case, and Noreen's testimony combined with the evidence was the slam dunk needed to make sure Baxter Heathcote didn't get away again.

The room had a soft glow, and the blinds were partially open. Noreen was sitting up in the bed, a glazed look in her eyes as she stared in the direction of the muted television in the corner of the room.

"Hey, Noreen," Shaylee said, moving to her side.

The woman slowly turned. "Shaylee. You're okay!"

She reached out her arms and Shaylee embraced her. A slight wince crossed Noreen's face, but she didn't complain. "How are you doing?"

"Ugh. Feels like I was shot and fell through a sinkhole," she joked.

Shaylee dragged a chair over and sat beside Noreen.

Jamey stood at the foot of the bed. "Do you remember anything?"

Noreen shook her head and pressed two fingers against her temple. "Moving causes my brain to hurt. No. I don't." Her lip quivered and her eyes remained fixed on Shaylee. "I'm so sorry."

"Shh. You tried to help us." Shaylee touched her hand. "I've arrested Baxter for shooting you."

"Then you know about everything, right?" Noreen glanced down and worked at biting a fingernail.

"I need to hear it from you, though," Shaylee said, waiting for Noreen to continue.

"It was like one of those snowball lies Grandma talked about. Everything spun out of control."

"Start at the beginning," Shaylee urged, holding Noreen's non-nail-biting hand.

"Zia threatened to go to the authorities with Baxter's accounting records. It was my job to protect him. Don't you see? I didn't want to hurt her. Honest. She wouldn't listen to me, though. I had to stop her."

Jamey's heart pounded. Shaylee's face remained neutral, conveying no emotion, but her unrelenting optimism and faith in Noreen's goodness would hold out until the last second.

"I talked to her, tried to explain what she was doing was wrong. I told her how great Baxter was for the community. I reasoned every possible way with her, but she refused to listen." Noreen's gaze bounced between Jamey and Shaylee. "You understand, right? Zia was his wife. She owed him her unwavering devotion! Yet she was the one who threatened to betray him by turning Baxter over to the authorities. I couldn't let that happen. He's a good man. He was going to do great things. He deserved a woman who would stand beside him through everything." She lifted her chin defiantly.

"A woman like you?" Jamey clarified.

Noreen addressed him as though she hadn't realized he was in the room. She tilted her head and spoke like he was a child. "Yes. I gave him time to grieve. That's the honorable thing to do. But I remained faithful to him."

"What did you do to Zia?" Shaylee asked.

Jamey heard the tension in her tone, but her expression remained stoic.

"I made the coffin for Zia as a way to scare her. She wasn't supposed to die. I knew once she had time to think about it, she'd agree not to go to the police with the accounting evidence. I worked hard on the design and buried it in the hills where no one would find her. Except she overdosed on the knockout drug and died on the way there," Noreen said as though that explained everything, and then resumed biting her fingernail.

Several long seconds passed.

"Was Baxter aware of your plan?" Jamey asked.

"Not at first. But when I got to the coffin, a group of campers was there. I didn't know what to do, so I called Baxter. He offered to help bury her in the valley and make the problem disappear. He's great at that."

Jamey caught sight of Shaylee's clenched jaw. "Why bury Shaylee, then? What had she done to deserve that?"

Shaylee hadn't said a word and he wanted to keep Noreen talking.

"She found the journal page and wouldn't leave Baxter alone. Just like Zia."

Shaylee stared at Noreen.

"I installed the camera so I could watch and make sure the blood-stained rags lured the coyotes to kill Shaylee if she got out of the coffin. But when you found her, the whole plan fell apart. Snowballs, you see?"

Noreen's rationalization almost made sense to Jamey. And it scared him. He glanced at Shaylee, who was seated with shoulders back, eyes probing. Her cop persona had returned.

"If you hadn't found the accounting page, it would've been forgotten. I didn't know Zia kept part of it until you showed up. Everything was unraveling."

"Baxter told you to handle it?" Jamey pressed.

"Yes. He was so angry." She looked down. "It's my fault. I should've destroyed the evidence, but I failed. He said I had to get rid of you, Shaylee. I researched how much of the knockout drug to give you." Noreen turned to Jamey. "Shaylee's stronger than me. I couldn't overpower her otherwise. And she had to be unconscious to get to the coffin. It was for the greater good, you see? I even had the park shelter rigged so Shaylee would set off the bomb with the trip wire after I'd left. That would've fixed the problem. But then Echo chased the geese and ruined it. Everything is a mess now."

Jamey fought the urge to let go of the railing. Noreen's justification for her actions was terrifying. "How did you find us today in the sinkhole?"

"Baxter and I traced you there." She frowned, creasing her forehead. "That's when I realized I'd messed up.

He planned to eliminate me, too. No loose ends. That's his motto."

"Noreen, why?" Shaylee gasped.

"Because it's my job to protect Baxter." The statement was so matter-of-fact it stunned Jamey.

"But we're like family," Shaylee said.

Noreen snorted. "No, we're not. You and Zia were real family. I was nothing more than the annoying little kid you had to take care of. But Baxter showed me how to be a woman. A respected professional. He loves me. You can only truly love one person. I asked you to walk away from the investigation. A true sister would've done that." Noreen's skewed sense of reality baffled Jamey.

Shaylee's cheeks flushed. Anger? Surely she saw what Noreen was trying to do?

Noreen looked down, fidgeting with the sheet. "Baxter trusted me to handle the problems. Take care of the details. I had to stop you before you traced the accounting journal to him. Wasn't I doing the right thing?"

"You lost sight of that a long time ago," Shaylee said.

Taken aback, Noreen said, "I'm sorry. Please forgive me."

Shaylee pushed back the chair and it crashed against the wall. "How can you ask that after all you've done?"

"You're right. I can't. I don't deserve it." Noreen continued twisting the sheet.

Jamey interrupted. "Noreen, what about the boots and shovel we found in the garden shed at your cabin?"

Her eyes widened. "The dog found them?" She spoke so low Jamey strained to hear her. "Baxter will be so angry. I should've thrown them away like he told me to." She bit on her fingernail again.

"Will we find your DNA inside those boots?" Shaylee's question held such hope, but Jamey was certain what Noreen's answer would be.

"They're mine. I told you Baxter was innocent. I just never told you I was guilty," Noreen concluded. "I love him. And love means protecting those you care about, at all costs. Just like you two have done from the beginning."

Jamey chased after Shaylee, catching up with her at the hospital doors. Dugan stayed in place, a look of confusion passing over his face.

"Noreen confessed to killing Zia," Jamey explained.

"Oh, I see." Dugan frowned. He glanced at Shaylee's heartbroken expression. "Shaylee believes the best about those she cares about. Almost to a fault. Go after her. I'll take care of these little ladies."

"Thank you."

Shaylee headed outside, and Jamey struggled to catch up with her. She stood beside her car, chest heaving. "How could she?" She turned to face him and the devastation in her eyes nearly undid him.

"I'm so sorry," Jamey said, taking her into his arms.

She allowed him to hold her while sobs racked her body. When she'd calmed enough to speak, she stepped back and looked up. "I trusted her."

He took her hand and led her to a bench. "Noreen needs help. She confused love and devotion to Baxter with her obsession for him. Her infatuation blinded her to the truth. She thought that since you loved Zia, you didn't love her."

Shaylee gaped at him. "That's what she meant when she said, 'You can only love one person'?"

"Yes."

"How could she do that? To Zia? To me?"

"In her mind, love motivated her actions. I'm in no way, shape or form justifying what she did. However, her reasons make perfect sense in her delusional state."

Shaylee shifted to face him.

He gently swiped a tear from her cheek.

"Love is a powerful motivator."

"Healthy love is. Noreen is obsessed. There's no excuse for what she did, and she'll pay for her crimes."

"Nobody won today. I've waited all this time to arrest Baxter. I did that, but I never thought Noreen would betray me. How could I have been so stupid?" Shaylee hiccupped.

"You believed in her based on your experience and history together. There's nothing wrong with that."

"I need to adopt your suspicious attitude. Would've saved me some heartache."

Jamey winced. "No. Please don't. Pessimism isn't fun and it's exhausting to be distrustful of everyone, all the time. Always thinking the worst. You've shown me a much better way to live. I want to be like you when I grow up."

Shaylee laughed. "There's a scary ambition. But I was blind. Just like Noreen with Baxter."

"Not a fair comparison. The difference between you and Noreen is ginormous, but in this particular example, you have the evidence. You're aware she has to pay for her crimes, you're not ignoring them. Sometimes loving someone means holding them accountable. Now Noreen will get the help she needs."

"God brought the truth to light," Shaylee said, squeezing Jamey's hand.

"Hey, I prayed that same thing a while ago."

"Great minds." She stood and Jamey joined her. They walked toward the hospital and paused near a stone column. "I'm glad you were there. I was so stunned when Noreen was talking, I couldn't speak."

"You did great." He gave her a hug. Jamey glanced down and spotted a cricket. "Watch out."

Shaylee jerked to look at him and stepped back, accidentally crushing the bug beneath her boot. "Ew." She shifted to the side.

"Never mind," he said. A thin black line emerged from the cricket. "Whoa. Zombie bug."

"Is that an entomological term of affection?" Shaylee asked, with a crooked grin.

"No, silly, just watch." Jamey pulled her close and pointed to the cricket as the rest of the worm emerged.

"And now I'm officially grossed out."

"But what a perfect illustration for what we're talking about. The horsehair worm, or *Spiochordodes tellinii*, enters the host, in this case the cricket, and takes over its brain by releasing a protein altering the cricket's central nervous system. It literally forces the bug to do its bidding."

Shaylee quirked a brow. "I don't know if I'm intrigued or confused. You've gotta be kidding."

"No. It's true. And like Noreen, the cricket is not in its right mind."

"You're saying Noreen is the host, and Baxter forced her to commit the crimes?"

Jamey snorted. "Not exactly. Baxter admitted he was aware of Noreen's feelings for him. We saw it plainly in that picture of the two of them. He took advantage of her naivety and vulnerability, using her to do his dirty work. He claimed to love her, manipulating Noreen, and she bought into it."

Shaylee pulled a tissue from her pocket and blew her nose. "Wow, as incredibly bizarre and disgusting as that correlation is, I totally get it. Her delusional perspective of 'love' forced her to protect him."

"Yes. And even real love can be blind. But it can also be a powerful incentive. It gave me the courage to keep fighting alongside you." Jamey's confession emerged before he stopped it.

Had he really said that aloud?

He swallowed hard. Why was his timing so incredibly bad?

Jamey searched his brain for something to say, for a follow-up that wouldn't put her on the spot, but his mouth went dry. Words eluded him.

She glanced up. "Jamey Dyer, are you saying you love me?"

He swallowed again. "Yes," he croaked. Ugh. "But I don't expect you to reciprocate. The timing is wrong. I had no right to blurt that—"

She pressed a finger to his lips. "Jamey, I love you, too."

He blinked. "You do?"

"Yes. I'm not sure when it happened, but it's like we've always known each other. And we make a really great crime-fighting team."

Jamey's heart thudded with delight. *Please don't say anything dumb.* He considered his next words carefully. "I agree wholeheartedly. You're an incredible woman, Shaylee Adler. I'm grateful our paths crossed. I realize this isn't the time. You're vulnerable, but I have to say this, or I might lose the courage to do so later."

Shaylee stepped back, her hands dropping to her side. "Fire when ready."

He grinned, his palms going damp. "I can't explain it, but I feel a connection with you like I've never had with anyone before. You changed me. As though finding you buried in the mountains completed a part of me that's always lacked. Is that wrong? It sounds so strange, but it was the best thing that ever happened to me." A chuckle of relief escaped.

Shaylee took both of his hands into hers. "How bizarre is it that I'm in total agreement? I mean, the Bible teaches God uses all things for good for those who love Him and are called to His purpose, but I'm not sure Paul meant that when he wrote the book of Romans."

"Is it corny to say we were meant to be together?"

"That's exactly it!" Shaylee encircled her arms around his neck and glanced up. "Declarations like that only happened in my cheesy rom-com movies."

"Can't say I've watched any of those. Educate me. What happens after the characters speak their affections for one another?" Jamey leaned in, pressing his hand against her lower back.

"They kiss, of course." Her words were breathless, warm on his cheeks.

Glancing over his shoulder, he caught sight of Captain Dugan approaching with the dogs. *Five more minutes, please.* "I can't imagine a moment without you." And now he had gone completely vulnerable, confessing everything. *Go ahead and lay it all out there.* "I don't do dating very well. This might come as a complete shock, but I'm awkward."

She quirked a brow. "No, say it ain't so," she teased.

He chuckled. "That obvious?"

"Little bit." Shaylee winked. "Are you trying to talk me into a relationship with you, or out of one?"

"Into one, definitely. And in my favor, I'm incredibly faithful. Ask Bugsy."

At her name, Bugsy barked and approached, tail wagging. Echo imitated her with two sharp barks.

"See?" Jamey laughed.

"On the affirmation of the dogs, I'd say you're trustworthy."

Jamey pulled her closer and brushed his lips across hers. The kiss was tender and soft. "We'll have the most unique 'how did you meet? story' to share. First I rescued you from a coffin, then Baxter tried to kill us a hundred different ways."

She laughed. "I think our grandchildren will love this story."

He sucked in a breath. She loved him, too. Where he'd had no hope of a real future before, the possibilities now loomed before him in an endless span of opportunities. Jamey squeezed her. "It'll be the stuff of legends in our family."

"Way to go, Bug Dude," Dugan whispered, giving Jamey a thumbs-up. Then, louder, he said, "See you at the office for that report, Adler."

She turned to face him but didn't let go of Jamey. "Yes, sir."

Jamey smiled. Maybe it was okay being Bug Dude.

EPILOGUE

Four months later

With Echo resting in her lap, Shaylee glanced up as Jamey and Bugsy entered Dugan's office. Her smile still sent his heart into rapid rhythms.

"Sorry I'm late." Jamey settled into the available chair with Bugsy beside him. "So, it's confirmed?"

Shaylee passed him a folder with documents. "The last of the test results arrived this morning. The blood on the boots was Zia's, and the soil samples prove they came from the sinkhole with traces of gypsum. DNA inside the boots confirms Noreen as the wearer."

"Baxter's trying to negotiate a plea deal, but the district attorney told Baxter's counsel to stop wasting their time. The DA's going for the maximum sentencing, and the media is blasting his deeds to the public. He couldn't get out of this mess with ten legal teams." Dugan leaned across the desk. "You were dead-on accurate, Jamey. Noreen's actions of placing Zia and the boots in Baxter's trunk left bug evidence even after she'd hidden them at the cabin."

"She'll have a long time to think about her crimes," Shaylee said, sadness in her tone.

Franny appeared in the doorway. "Y'all should get a move on."

Shaylee glanced at her watch. "Oops, she's right."

The group relocated to the press conference in the city council chambers. Jamey and Shaylee took their place behind the podium where Dugan repeated the charges against Noreen and Baxter along with the status updates.

The governor stepped forward. "We owe a debt of gratitude to Jamey Dyer and his forensic detection canine, Bugsy, for rescuing Detective Adler. Without their keen partnership and skilled training, she would've died at the hands of Noreen Liddle and Baxter Heathcote. Additionally, their efforts resulted in the discovery of Zia Heathcote's remains. In appreciation for all their work, I'm proud to name them this year's Governor's Honor recipients."

Dugan provided closing remarks.

Afterward, while Shaylee and Jamey mingled, his old boss, George Pritchard, approached. "Dyer, I owe you an apology. If you're willing, your job is yours for the taking."

"I appreciate the offer, but I've got other plans." Jamey put an arm around Shaylee.

"Understandable. Best to you." George smiled.

"Please excuse us." Jamey led Shaylee outside and together they strolled the city grounds to a stone bench under a maple tree. He'd wanted a romantic setting, but he'd burst if he waited a second longer.

"Look!" Shaylee pointed at two orange-and-black spotted butterflies flitting by. "Regal fritillary."

He gaped. "You remember their name?"

She shrugged. "You're a great teacher."

Love warmed his heart to overflowing. *God, thank You for the privilege of loving this woman. Give me the courage to ask her.*

"And if I'm not mistaken, he's courting her," Shaylee said.

Sure enough, the male chased the female in circular flight, dancing above the wildflowers. He glanced down at

Bugsy, who winked and panted contentedly. Echo barked, tail wagging, as if to say, *Now!*

Jamey sucked in a breath. "Shaylee, the day you entered into my life, I realized I'd missed out on everything I never knew I wanted." He was rambling. "Um, I mean. Why am I so nervous? This sounded so much better in my head."

She grinned, a knowing sparkle in her eyes. "Just say it really fast."

He swiped a sweaty palm against his pants and removed the ring he'd carried in his pocket for two weeks. He displayed the solitaire between his thumb and forefinger. "Shaylee Adler, would you do me the honor of becoming Mrs. Bug Dude?"

She threw herself into his arms and he nearly dropped the ring. "Yes!"

Jamey kissed her deeply, inhaling the scent of her perfumed shampoo.

"Hey, what's with the PDA?" Dugan's voice boomed, interrupting the moment.

"A totally justifiable reason for a public display of affection," Shaylee interpreted, though Jamey understood the acronym. He slipped the ring onto her finger.

"He finally asked?" Dugan grinned.

Shaylee blinked. "You knew?"

"Since the captain is family to you, I felt it appropriate to ask him first for your hand in marriage," Jamey explained.

Shaylee chuckled. "What if he'd said no?"

Dugan cleared his throat, and Jamey swallowed hard. "I would've had to beg Bugsy to convince him."

Shaylee laughed.

Dugan slapped Jamey's shoulder a little harder than necessary. "I can't think of a better man. You have my blessing."

Shaylee smiled wider. "Great, because I need to give you my resignation."

Dugan frowned. "What?"

"Jamey and I are opening a private investigation agency specializing in multiple canine disciplines like search and rescue, forensic and detection. Along with Jamey's entomology experience."

"After the wedding and a long honeymoon," Jamey inserted.

Shaylee's cheeks blushed. "Definitely."

Dugan met his eyes. "Bug Dude returns?"

"Proudly, sir." Jamey laughed.

"Brilliant plan." Dugan leaned to pet Bugsy and Echo. "If you'll teach an old dog like me to work with one of these awesome creatures, I might ask for a job."

"You hold the leash, and they do the work," Jamey said.

"Sign me up." Dugan winked before walking away.

"This morning I read that God restores the years the locusts have stolen. I don't know if that applies to us, but it spoke to me. Just like God turning ashes into beauty."

Shaylee kissed him softly. "He doesn't waste anything. Not tears, or pain, or loss. Somehow it works together for His perfect plan."

* * * * *

Dear Reader,

I hope you enjoyed the journey through Black Hills National Forest with Jamey, Shaylee, Bugsy and Echo. I had the incredible pleasure of visiting Black Hills National Forest in South Dakota to research this book. It's truly one of the most beautiful places I've ever seen.

Research is one of my favorite parts of writing a story, and I'm often asked where I get ideas. They come from all over the place, usually unexpectedly. Actual sinkholes were found in Black Hawk, South Dakota, and reading about them inspired this story. The insect references and details were a little bit gross, but I admit, they were fascinating, too.

I am continually amazed by God's creativity in nature. The intricate details of every living thing, of the landscape, and the beauty of animals like Bugsy and Echo. All of it points to what an awesome God we serve.

I love hearing from readers! You can find me on social media or email me at authorshareestover@gmail.com. But the best way to keep in touch with me and get the inside scoop on my books is to join my newsletter. You can find the sign-up link at my website, www.shareestover.com.

Many blessings to you,
Sharee